John E Lawrence is new to the world of writing fiction. He founded his health and safety consultancy more than fourteen years ago, providing specialist health, safety and fire safety engineering advice to the construction industry and the built environment.

In 2019, he handed down the daily management of the business to his son, Tom, allowing him to pursue his other interests.

He started on his journey, writing fiction in 2020, just before the pandemic hit the UK, completing his first novel *The Heroes* at the beginning of 2021.

John has been married for over thirty years and lives with his wife in their family home on the Sussex Coast of England.

To my wife, Allison, who has supported me.

John E Lawrence

THE HEROES

AUST**I**N MACAULEY PUBLISHERS™

LONDON * CAMBRIDGE * NEW YORK * SHARJAH

A CIP catalogue record for this title is available from the British Library.

ISBN 9781398460904 (Paperback)
ISBN 9781398460911 (Hardback)
ISBN 9781398460935 (ePub e-book)
ISBN 9781398460928 (Audiobook)

www.austinmacauley.com

First Published 2023
Austin Macauley Publishers Ltd®
1 Canada Square
Canary Wharf
London
E14 5AA

A big thank you to Jericho Writers, Thomas Lawrence, Hazel Mattock, Simon Ingram, and Paula Jackson for their help, guidance, and encouragement.

Table of Contents

Chapter 1

The woman dressed in body-hugging black Nike running gear, stopped outside of the black entrance door, next to the hat shop in the Lanes, in Brighton Square. Familiar with the coded keypad, she punched in the entry door code for 'Fox and Bennett – Private Detective Agency'.

"Best if you wait in the shop," she said to the other woman with her.

The buzzer sounded, the locking mechanism clicked, and the woman pushed the door open, stepped inside and climbed the stairs in front of her to the first-floor landing. Looking to her right, on the opaque half-glazed panelled door was a sign—written in black, with the words 'Fox and Bennett'.

She pushed the door open and let herself in. The Venetian blinds across the windows were open, and sunlight filled the room, illuminating the top of the two mahogany desks positioned opposite each other on either side of the room. One was piled high in papers and ring binder folders, the other clear and neatly set out with a business card holder on its right, blotter pad with a writing pad on top in its centre, and a phone on the left. A three-seater settee was positioned with its back against the window, and another door was tucked away in the far corner of the room.

Behind her came a familiar voice.

"Hello, Tegan. Come to check up on me, have you?"

Tegan turned to see Rosemary Bennett striding towards her with a tray of refreshments in her hands, the smell of fresh coffee replacing the stale air of the stairwell.

"Morning, Rosemary," Tegan replied cheerfully, holding the door open, allowing Rosemary to pass her and place the tray on the clear desk. "I was hoping to see your new partner, Robert Fox. I have someone in the shop who is looking for you both."

"You are unlucky today, Tegan, I'm afraid. He's in London on business and I'm just off to an appointment."

"Shame," replied Tegan, showing her disappointment at not meeting Robert. "He's been with you for nearly a year now, hasn't he?"

"He has indeed, and he has fitted right in," replied Rosemary.

"Got his name on the door, I see, Rose, I mean Rosemary," Tegan corrected herself.

Rosemary didn't reply, so Tegan continued.

"I've been for a run along the seafront, this morning, where I joined a group of runners, one of which was telling me about wanting to find her brother's headmaster, who she says is missing. Apparently, everyone has told her that he's dead, but she's not convinced. She didn't say much more, just that she could do with some help from a local private investigator."

"Has she been to the police?" Rosemary asked.

"Apparently so, they too have confirmed that he is probably dead. So, I told her about you and Robert. You know how I like to help local businesses in need, so I thought you might be able to help her," suggested Tegan. "Her name is Jayne."

"I can certainly have a word, Tegan," responded Rosemary, grabbing a business card from the desk behind her, and passing it to her uninvited guest, said, "Ask her to call me when she can, and I shall be happy to talk to her."

"Oh…I thought that you would like to talk to her now."

"Now?" Rosemary replied, irritated at the fact that Tegan was now trying to organise her diary.

"Well, yes, no time like the present, is there? She is waiting downstairs, in the shop, and she was very insistent that she came to see you, now."

"Really, Tegan?" replied Rosemary, trying not to lose her cool with her landlord's wife. "I do have another appointment at ten-thirty."

"Well, I'm sure this meeting won't take long. I'll get her now," Tegan replied. She paced quickly out of the office and bound down the stairs. Rosemary didn't hear the entrance door close shut.

I need to complain to Tegan's husband about her just letting herself in without asking, she thought.

Rosemary busied herself by positioning a single chair in front of her desk, ready for the unknown guest, then checking herself in the full-length mirror which hung behind the office door, smoothing down her white blouse, then twisting the waistline of her grey knee-length skirt around, so that the side seams of her skirt were correctly positioned at her side, she stood in front of her desk waiting to greet her potential new client.

She heard the front entrance door creak open, then slam closed shut, followed by the stomp of two pairs of feet climbing the stairs.

Tegan stood to one side of the office doorway, allowing Jayne to enter the room.

"Rose, this is Jayne. I told her that you would be able to help her."

Jayne was five-ten tall and slim, her body shape hidden beneath her black baggy jogging outfit, unlike Tegan, who enjoyed flaunting hers.

Rosemary took a step forward and held out her hand, which Jayne shook. "Hello, I'm Rosemary Bennett. How can I be of assistance?"

"I think I'm in need of your help, Rosemary. My name is Jayne Sargeant. I would like you to help me find the headmaster of Plumpton Primary School because he has disappeared, and I believe that his disappearance was because he stumbled on to something rather sinister to do with the death of my brother, Derek."

"Have a seat, Jayne. Alright if I call you Jayne?"

"Yes," Jayne replied, taking the seat offered to her. Tegan remained standing in the doorway.

"When did the headmaster disappear?" Rosemary asked.

"1968," Jayne replied.

"1968?" Tegan blurted out, "That's more than fifty years ago."

"Tegan. Thank you," scolded Rosemary, realising that she was still in earshot. "I will take it from here, thank you," she continued, as she walked over to the door, ushering Tegan out of the doorway, and then watched her descend the staircase, opening the door onto the alleyway.

"Can you make sure that the entrance door is closed behind you, please? Thank you."

Tegan slammed the door shut, and Rosemary returned to her office, closing the door behind her. Stepping around to her side of the desk, Rosemary continued the conversation.

"You were saying, Jayne."

"You are the first person who hasn't reacted the way that Tegan just did when I told them about the year in which he disappeared."

Rosemary poured coffee for them both. "What about the police?" Rosemary asked.

"They're of the opinion that as he hasn't been seen for more than ten years, they have declared him dead," Jayne replied.

"What does the headmaster have to do with your brother?"

"He was my stepbrother. My mother told me that Derek died suddenly in his teacher's arms in the playground at the school, on the day when they announced that the headmaster had committed suicide."

Jayne unzipped her hip bag and teased out a monochrome print.

"Derek died six months after this class photo was taken," said Jayne, pointing to her stepbrother seated amongst school children, in front a brick and flint wall. "His death was recorded as heart failure, but my mother maintained that he was in the best of health, and then there was the headmaster's note to her."

Jayne handed over a triangular-shaped piece of paper which had been torn on the diagonal, on which there was a handwritten note, to Rosemary.

Rosemary read it out loud.

"Karen, I'm sorry. Peter."

"Do you know Peter's full name?" Rosemary asked.

"Peter Dennett," Jayne replied.

"Do you or your mother know what he meant when he said sorry?"

"No, we don't. My mother is in her eighties, she doesn't remember too much nowadays, but she does remember the day my brother died."

"When did she receive the note?"

"She found it in Derek's old scrapbook photo album, when we cleared out the loft, six weeks ago. My mother is moving into a care home at the end of the month. I took the note to the police, but they took no notice. They told me that he had probably committed suicide by jumping from Beachy Head."

"What evidence do the police have to confirm their presumption that he died?"

"They told me that the archive reports state that he was suffering from severe stress at the time when they discovered his car at the top of Beachy Head and surmised that he had committed suicide."

"Can I presume that no body was found?" asked Rosemary.

"No, and it never has," replied Jayne.

"Would you like me to find Peter Dennett?" Rosemary asked.

"Not just find him, Miss Bennett. I would like to know why he disappeared so suddenly, what caused him to go missing and never be found. I would also like to know why he put the note in the album, whether he is in fact dead or alive, and if he is alive, then where is he?"

"Why come to us now, Jayne?"

"It's my mother's final wish, so I'd rather engage you, if you have the time, so that I can spend what precious days I have left with her."

"Do you have the album with you, Jayne?"

"I don't, my mother keeps it with her. It's the only tangible link between her and Derek. I can arrange for you to have a look at it in a couple of days."

"Is there anything other than the photo which may help our enquiries?"

"Unfortunately, no."

"That's fine, then we can start with what we have immediately, Jayne. We shall endeavour to find out all about Peter Dennett, but as you can appreciate, there are no guarantees that we'll find the answers that you are hoping for."

"I understand. I shall leave the photo and the note with you. Good luck Rosemary, and I hope to hear from you in the next few days."

Jayne rose from her seat placing the cup and saucer on the desk, as did Rosemary, they shook hands and Jayne said, "I shall see myself out," and left the office, closing the door behind her.

Rosemary heard Jayne descend the stairs, then the door creak open and slam shut.

Rosemary checked that the stairwell was empty and returning to her office, sat back down in her chair and studied the photo.

She grabbed her phone and called her partner in her investigation practice, Robert Fox, to tell him about their new client. He told her that he was working with one of his old colleagues in London, that he'd be staying overnight and that he would call her in the morning. She smiled to herself when he ended the call with his now-familiar departing phrase, "Signing Off."

She signed into her computer, opened a browser, and typed in Plumpton Green Primary School.

There were several entries. She chose Plumpton Historic Society. On the menu, she pressed 'Gallery'. The image on the screen in front of her showed four women sitting around a table with a man seated at one end.

Under the photo, it gave their names, Peter Dennett, Karen Sargeant, Teresa Johnson, Jean Field, and Charlotte Embling. She printed off the photo, then set it down next to the monochrome image given to her by Jayne and confirmed to herself that the teacher sitting in the middle of the classroom of boys and girls was the same as Charlotte Embling sitting at the table.

Rosemary typed in 'the British Newspaper Archive', into the browser which has over forty million archived articles online. Entering Plumpton Primary School, on one tab and Charlotte Embling on another, she found the address she was looking for.

"Look forward to meeting you tomorrow, Charlotte."

Chapter 2

Rosemary Bennett watched the elderly woman tilling the sandy soil in the flowerbed, in front of her bungalow. "Hi there," called Rosemary, gaining the woman's attention, "I'm looking for Charlotte Embling." The elderly woman stood unsteadily on her feet and walked over to the gate. *A very elegant lady*, Rosemary thought, seeing the old woman's long silver hair grown down to her waistline, gently blowing in the cool breeze.

Charlotte hesitated before responding, her thoughts suddenly spiralling back more than fifty years. She hadn't been known by her maiden name for years. To her neighbours, she was Charlotte Jackson. She contemplated her response, before giving her reply. "No one by that name here, young lady, sorry."

"Do you know where I may find her?" Rosemary asked, "I was hoping that she could help me with my enquiries."

"Are you the police?"

"No, I'm a private Investigator. I believe that she can help me find somebody."

"May I ask who?"

"That information is between me and Miss Embling."

"I am intrigued as to why you think she may live here. Who gave you this address, Miss…?"

"Miss Bennett, Rosemary Bennett. This is her family home according to the census of 1968 and I was given this snapshot of Miss Embling in this class photo," responded Rosemary, holding it up in front of Charlotte. The photo in front of her was younger, but there was no mistaking the likeness, and she knew her visitor saw the resemblance too.

"You know, I haven't gone by the name of Charlotte Embling since I was married back in 1974," she replied to Rosemary.

Rosemary, in a quiet voice, said, "I presume then, Mrs Jackson, that you know Peter Dennett?"

"The Peter Dennett that I knew was once the headmaster of Plumpton Primary School."

"Could we talk about him and the photo I have with me, please?" asked Rosemary.

Charlotte stared at the photo in Rosemary's hand and remembered sitting in the middle of a group of children in front of the entrance to Plumpton Primary School, for the annual class photo. "You're looking for Mr Dennett, you say?" asked Charlotte.

"Yes, I believe that you were a teacher at the school when he disappeared." Charlotte looked warily at Rosemary, pondering whether she should talk to this stranger about her past, and then she shuddered, losing her balance, as her own comment struck her. *Is Peter Dennett still alive?* she thought.

Rosemary noticed her hesitation.

"Is he alive?" Charlotte questioned.

"That's what I'm trying to find out."

"For whom, may I ask?"

"The sister of this boy in this photo," replied Rosemary, pointing to Derek Sargeant.

Charlotte's expression changed in an instant, to one of confusion.

"Derek didn't have a sister," Charlotte announced.

"Oh, but he did. She was born after he died," Rosemary replied, grabbing at Charlotte's interest.

"Why does she want to know what happened to Peter Dennett?"

"She doesn't; her mother does."

"Karen? She had a daughter? I never knew."

"It's not common knowledge."

Charlotte wobbled unsteadily on her feet, grabbing on to the gate between them to steady herself.

"Are you okay? Can I help you inside?" asked Rosemary.

She saw Charlotte take a couple of deep breaths.

"I think that would be a good idea," Charlotte replied. Rosemary led Charlotte into her home with her arm under hers, closing the front door behind them, and leading her through the corridor to a room, where she sat her on one of the oak chairs positioned around the round oak table. She quickly scanned the room. The lounge-diner was sparse with two sideboards, just one settee, two matching floral armchairs and the round oak dining table they sat at, surrounded by four chairs. She watched Charlotte take a few deep breaths.

"Thank you," Charlotte said, "you're very kind." Charlotte and Rosemary sat opposite each other at the table with the old photograph that Rosemary had brought with her, between them.

"Can you tell me about this photo?" asked Rosemary.

Charlotte hesitated, thinking back to her time at the school.

"This is you, isn't it?" Rosemary asked, pointing at the young teacher in the middle of the children.

"Yes. It was 1968. I remember it as if it were yesterday," recollected Charlotte, as she ran her right hand through her long silvery hair, whilst gazing at the school photo of Class 3EM. "I loved teaching all the children in this photo, but I had my favourites, you know, as all teachers have. Mine were these five schoolboys sitting together. I affectionately named them as 'The Heroes' of Plumpton Primary School" – Charlotte recounted, pointing at each of the boys in turn – "because they all volunteered to retrieve their beloved football, when it had been accidentally kicked over the playground's high chain-link fence, from the stream during the school lunch breaks. The shallow stream, which meandered alongside the school's northwest boundary, slowly flowed towards Lewes, where it joined the River Ouse. It still does; however, the school is long gone. It was a funny sight, seeing the boys scaling over the high fence, them being just five years of age. Boys took risks in those days, nowadays, they don't, and it was fabulous seeing them scaling the fence as they matured in age, especially when the boys were all the age of eight. It took them much less effort and little time to climb over the playground boundary, retrieve the ball and re-join their cohorts before they were caught red-handed by the other teachers or their assistants." Charlotte tittered to herself. "The ball retrieval had always been a covert and exciting activity carried out by the boys, largely without incident, usually coinciding with a staged fight which was played out at the southern end of the tarmac playground. The fight diverted the attention away from the true goal of retrieving their beloved football. I know I should have stopped them climbing the fence, it was always a bit risky, but none of them ever fell, and they were my favourites. I made sure that I was always there to catch them if they were to fall, and as I've said, the stream was not fast flowing or deep." Again, Charlotte tittered. "I remember that the punishment for the boys being caught outside of the school boundary was expulsion for the remainder of the week, sometimes two, plus, of course, the obligatory meeting with the parents, none of which any of the boys wanted. The tell-tale signs of their infringement, other than being caught in the act, had been when they had lost their footing and had slipped on the moss-covered banks into the slow-running shallow stream. There weren't many occasions, but when they did slip, I was the teacher responsible for placing their wet clothes on to the radiators in the school staff room."

Charlotte paused for a moment, then continued.

"All but one of 'the heroes' had slipped into the meandering stream in the first week of spring term of that year, two on the same day and were punished by expulsion for a week in which time they had all contracted flu. Their parents complained incessantly to the Governors of the school, saying that we weren't taking care of them during school time and that the school's security arrangements were severely lacking. The complaints rapidly subsided when any football games during breaks had been banned by the school, two weeks afterwards on the direction of the Education Authority, to the displeasure of all of the boys in the school." Charlotte focused her eyes again, on the five boys in the photograph in turn. "It was the day after the ban that there was an unexpected and sudden arrival of men and women in white laboratory coats, in their waders, taking water samples along the stream.

"The kids couldn't take their eyes off them, pressing their noses up against the fence for a better view, although the visit was short.

"It was a couple of days later that the northern end of the playground was separated from the school with another shrouded high-level chain-link fence. The security personnel in battle fatigues were posted at the entrance gate onto the highway at the front of the school and a convoy of mobile cabins were wheeled into the enclosure."

"What did Peter Dennett make of all of this disruption to the school?" Rosemary asked, trying to steer the conversation towards finding out about the headmaster.

"Poor Mr Dennett, the school's Headmaster seemed keen to involve the pupils of the school with the unusual activities going on behind the fence. He proclaimed himself editor of the school magazine, which he named 'The Meander', its name derived from the meandering stream of course, which he was due to publish, but the small paper was confiscated by the Education Authority that very morning from the school, before it was circulated.

"He didn't attend school that day, or any day after that, which took us all by surprise. We were told the very next day, in his office by the Chair of Governors, that he had gone missing and a week later he was presumed dead. His car was found at the top of the cliff at Beachy Head. His body was never found, and many surmised that he had committed suicide. Personally, I do not believe he could do that."

Rosemary reflected on the conversation with Jayne, and it seemed to coincide with Charlotte's account. "On that tragic day, when we learnt about Mr Dennett's apparent demise, the five heroes" – Charlotte said, pointing to each of the boys in turn – "John, Keith, Alan, Trevor, and Derek, were playing tag with each other in the playground. Derek had been complaining to me earlier that morning of feeling unwell, and his mother had been called to collect him as soon as she could. He perked up a bit at morning break and was happily running around through the crowded playground, ducking behind a group of boys gathered around two opponents playing conker fights and another group of girls playing hopscotch. Towards the end of the break, I could sense that Derek wasn't right. His speech was slurred, and his body movements became robotic. I remember quickly pacing towards him, the mass of children parting, forming a clear pathway for me, as I strode directly towards him. He saw me coming and he ran directly into my open arms. I will never forget the horror on his face, his eyes staring up at me, then the sudden fitting of his body as he fell into my arms, his dead weight pulling me to the ground, and grabbing hold of his jumper at his chest with his right hand, he gasped, 'the spacemen' with his last breath. I saw his eyes roll back into his head and felt his boiling sweaty body go limp. I cradled his sodden, clothed, lifeless body in my arms, tears streaming down my cheeks as I cried out for help." Charlotte paused to gain another deep breath. Rosemary's lips were pursed as she held Charlotte's gaze, listening intently to the tragic events unfolding.

Charlotte's soulful eyes locked with Rosemary's and said, "I couldn't save him you know; he died in my arms. Those poor children were standing around me, the other teachers asking if Derek and I were alright, and then Derek's mother appeared in front of me and saw me sitting on the ground, with her dead son in my arms. I didn't know what to say. All I could say was 'I'm so sorry'. The look of disbelief, a look that only a mother makes when she knows the worst has happened. That look will be etched on my mind forever." Charlotte broke down sobbing quietly, her head bowed, the tears now flooding over her flushed cheeks. Rosemary looked at the pensioner's silver hair falling to each side of her face, patiently waiting for Charlotte to recompose herself. After a few minutes, Charlotte raised her head and stroked her long hair away from her face. "I'm sorry. What must you think of me?" she asked, as she palmed the tears from her face.

"Charlotte, the last thing I wanted was to upset you," Rosemary said.

"I haven't spoken about the past for many years, not until you turned up at my door," replied Charlotte, "in fact, I haven't spoken to anybody for a long time." She paused, regaining her thoughts. "I felt sorrier for Derek's mother. They didn't release his body from the mortuary for over a month. It must have been torturous for his mother. He was her only child. They told her it was because they had to do a post-mortem, not once but twice. They, the health authority, said he had died from a heart attack that could have happened at any time, apparently from an underlying health condition that had never been picked up previously. His school friends were traumatised, blaming themselves for making him run after them around the farmer's barns and fields on the previous night. They told me that 'the spacemen' were chasing them, but when I enquired, everyone in the village told me that it was their imagination running away with them. I kept reminding the boys that it wasn't their fault" – Charlotte again paused for a few moments, then continued – "I left the school shortly afterwards and teaching in this country, for that matter. I have never forgotten that day, and never will."

"Have you kept track of the others?" asked Rosemary, as she looked carefully into her eyes.

"The others?"

"Yes, John, Keith, Alan and Trevor."

"The Heroes," Charlotte replied. "What teacher doesn't remember the children in their care? I can tell you now that they all excelled in their schooling and have forged their own successful careers."

"Do they contact you, or you contact them at all nowadays, Charlotte?" Rosemary saw Charlotte smile and her eyes dart upper left, signifying that she was remembering happier times again.

"I bumped into Trevor just last week in Oxford Street, literally, when I was going into Selfridges. He was very sweet, and I was elated when he immediately recognised me, after all these years, and called me Miss Embling. He was coming out of the department store, having bought his wife a beautiful vase for her birthday. He nearly dropped the bag that it was in when we collided as I entered the store. I didn't recognise him at first, but as soon as he called out my name and mentioned his and Plumpton School, the memories came flooding back, and now," she hesitated, then continued, "you are talking to me about my time at the school." Charlotte suddenly looked concerned. Rosemary could see the change in Charlotte's facial expression. She knew she had to get more information from the only other real lead she had in finding out about Peter Dennett.

"So, how was Trevor?"

"Oh, he is very well. He is so tall, so handsome and he has one of those fashionable sculptured beards. We went for coffee in the new restaurant on the first floor of Selfridges. Now, what was it called?" she asked, as she raised her eyes to the ceiling, scanning her memory for the answer.

"The Brasserie of Lights," Rosemary replied.

"Yes, that's it. Have you been there too?"

"I have been there a few times," replied Rosemary.

"It's beautiful. We sat directly under the silver Pegasus."

"I remember sitting there too; it is beautiful," responded Rosemary. "Does he live close by the restaurant, do you know?" Rosemary asked.

"I'm not sure. My knowledge of London is not the best," Charlotte replied, "but he works in an office in Green Park, just along from Annabel's Wine Bar, he told me. He must be doing very well for himself. He was wearing a very expensive suit and that vase that he bought for his wife must have cost him over a thousand pounds!"

"Wow," replied Rosemary, committing Charlotte's response to memory. "You must have felt so proud of Trevor when you met up with him."

"Oh yes, I was, and I am. I was just trying to work out how old he is now because he was eight when I was twenty-two."

"That would mean that he is fifty-nine now," Rosemary replied.

Charlotte nodded. "How time flies," she muttered.

"Can I use your bathroom please?" requested Rosemary.

Charlotte nodded and led the way out of the lounge-diner and pointed to the door in the corridor to her left. Rosemary snibbed the lock on the toilet door, took her iPhone from her pocket and fired off a quick text confirming Trevor's whereabouts. Just as she re-entered the lounge, a text message pinged up on her phone. She quickly glanced at the response. 'Message received. Be in Green Park within the hour. Signing off.' Charlotte was seated at the table. Rosemary could sense that Charlotte had something on her mind. "Now, where were we?" Rosemary asked.

Charlotte hesitated for a moment, then questioned, "How did you find me?"

"I found your parent's address from the local papers and took a chance that you might still live here," replied Rosemary.

"I haven't lived in England for many years, as I said, I left at the end of the academic year of 1968 and returned just over two years ago."

"I also found some information which may interest you too, in the register of births, deaths and marriages," Rosemary said, showing Charlotte the certificate. "Did you know that Peter Dennett fathered a daughter named Abigail?"

"No. When was this?" Charlotte asked, "He would have told me he had a daughter. His wife couldn't have children, and she died a couple of years before he came to the school."

"He had a secret liaison during his time at the school, apparently," clarified Rosemary, "his daughter was born six months after his disappearance, so he would never have known."

"A liaison with whom?" Charlotte asked.

"Mrs Wilton."

"Keith's mum? Does Keith know?" asked Charlotte.

"I wouldn't know, but if he doesn't, he should be told."

Chapter 3

The shiny black Range Rover blended in with the other luxurious vehicles parked in Hill Street outside the 'Coach and Horses' pub. It had taken just fifteen minutes to travel to Green Park following a tip-off, and since its arrival, the team of three men and one woman had busied themselves making enquiries about Trevor Johnson. One of the male passengers scouted the area for possible locations of his whereabouts. The woman stepped out of the front passenger door and set foot in the pub as soon as they had arrived. Rachel's tall slim body had attracted all the attention, as soon as she stepped through the door, her long naked slender legs beneath her miniskirt, striding purposefully to the near-empty bar.

"Hi, I'm looking for Trevor Johnson."

"You're a tad early, sweetheart," said the barman, eyeing her up and down. "He doesn't usually get here till half-past twelve. Is he expecting you?"

"Course he is," came the slurred reply from the inebriated man sitting at the end of the bar. "Always one for the ladies is Trevor, especially the pretty ones."

"Why thank you, young man," replied Rachel, flashing her broad smile as she side-stepped closer to him, "and what can I get for you on this fine morning?"

"I'm liking you already, love," said the old man, glaring at her cleavage. "Compliments and a free drink; must be my lucky day. Well, as you're offering, mine's a pint, please." He pointed to the draught bitter, giving the barman the signal to serve him.

"I want to surprise him," Rachel whispered so only he could hear. "Where can I find him?"

The barman placed the man's beer in front of him. "And for you, Miss?" the barman asked.

"Nothing for me, just information," Rachel replied.

The drunk sitting next to her nodded to Rachel to express his thanks for the drink. "He'll be in his office, just around the corner. He'll love a pretty thing like you turning up on his doorstep, especially looking like that."

Rachel placed her hand on his knee and gently squeezed, sending a rare tingle through his body, causing him to cough into his beer. "Thank you," she whispered.

"The pleasure's all mine, love," he replied, with a broad grin on his face.

Rachel turned to face the polished walnut bar, placed a ten-pound note on the surface. "Keep the change," she announced to the barman, then winked at the man, turned on her heels and left.

She stepped out onto Hill Street, crossed the road, and slid into the front passenger seat of the Range Rover, where she grabbed the change of clothing from the driver, quickly changed her miniskirt for a formal grey skirt and re-buttoned her white blouse. She fashioned her hair into a bun, checking her image using the sun visor's mirror. The men knew better than to speak whilst she changed. They all knew that she had a vicious temper.

She smiled at herself, knowing that she had authority over the other occupants, and without looking away from the mirror said, "He has an office in Hays Mews," to which Brad in the rear seat confirmed, "The brass plate at Number Fouteen has his name on it."

"Good work," she replied, her eyes focusing on him in the mirror to see him smile.

"Thanks, boss," he replied.

She turned to her driver. "Wait for me outside when I give the signal; you all know the drill." She donned her suit jacket and grabbing the black clipboard from the centre console, swung the car's door open and stepped down onto the pavement.

The passengers' eyes locked on to her gently swaying hips, as she paced down Hill Street, disappearing from their view as she made a right into Hays Mews. "Bet she's commanding in bed," Brad said aloud, making the others snigger.

"Don't let her hear you say that; it's just not worth it," replied the driver as he slowly pulled away from the kerb rounding the corner into the Mews, stopping at the rear of Annabel's Wine Bar, waiting for her signal to meet her outside Number Fourteen's door, which was thirty metres down the road.

Rachel's comms picked up Brad's comment, but she decided to ignore it for now, and focusing on the task, she stepped over the threshold into Number Fourteen.

The receptionist greeted Rachel with a wide smile and beckoned Trevor from his office to meet his visitor.

She was used to pretty women turning up around an hour before the office lunch break, accompanying him to his private office on the first floor, and then him whisking them away from the office for two to three hours.

Rachel quickly scanned the crisp white folders on the reception desk and spotted a company name that she knew well.

Trevor bound down the last eight treads of the spiral staircase, landing lightly on the natural granite tiled floor, before striding, arm outstretched to shake hands with the unexpected and extremely attractive visitor.

"Good morning, Trevor Johnson and how may—"

Rachel interrupted his introduction, "Kim Selby of Carruthers and Crowther. Can I have a quiet word with you, please?"

The century-old solicitors, Carruthers and Crowther, was one of his most affluent clients, but he hadn't met Kim Selby before, although he'd wished he had.

He motioned to the boardroom door to his left.

"Outside, if that's okay?" She turned and walked towards the front door, depressing the click switch in the palm of her left hand to alert her driver as soon as Trevor started to follow her.

The Range Rover came to a stop against the kerb of the pavement, outside of Number Fourteen, the two men springing from the rear of the vehicle to stand behind Rachel's and Trevor's line of vision. Rachel pointed down the road towards the newly glazed structure in the corner, diverting his attention away from the extraction team behind them. With practised and well-rehearsed precision, Midazolam was injected into Trevor's neck just above the collar, as Rachel opened the nearside rear door, allowing the two men to bundle him into the car, wedging him between them. Rachel shut the rear door and opening the front nearside door, slid into the front passenger seat. The amnesiac drug worked on Trevor almost immediately, inducing drowsiness.

The vehicle sped off to the junction, taking a right into Chesterfield Hill, narrowly missing the black Ford Galaxy, which was about to make a right turn into Hays Mews.

Robert slammed on the brakes, just as his offside wheel hit a pothole in the road, bringing the Galaxy to an abrupt halt. The sudden jerk of the car caused the dash cam attached to his front windscreen to double bleep, recording the incident as a collision. He stared at the female passenger who mouthed "Sorry", as he was about to mouth expletives at her, but thought better of it. Their eyes locked together for the briefest of seconds, but enough for Robert to commit the woman's sultry look to memory.

The Range Rover's tyres screeched on the tarmac as it sped up the road, before it made a sharp left turn into Hill Street and was gone. Robert continued into Hays Mews and stopped outside Number Fourteen.

Opening his door onto the pavement, he stepped out from his car and rang the entry door buzzer. The door lock clicked open, and he stepped inside the reception area.

"Hello Isobel," he said cheerily, spying her name badge. "I'm here to see Trevor Johnson. My name is Robert Fox."

"I'm afraid you've just missed him," the Receptionist replied, "Literally a minute earlier and you would have caught him before he left the office with one of his clients."

Robert noted that no names had been entered into the visitors' register on the desktop that morning.

"Do you know where he was headed, Isobel?"

"No, however, he is expected to return here at around 3 pm this afternoon."

"It's urgent that I get a message to him, Isobel. Can I reach him on his mobile? I would be grateful for your assistance."

"Mobile numbers aren't given out, I'm afraid," Isobel responded.

Robert pressed on to gain more information, "His assistance with my enquiries would be appreciated."

"Are you Police?" she enquired.

"No, I'm a private investigator, Isobel, and it is essential that I talk to him. Can you ask him to call me please as soon as he can? Here's my card." He handed her his business card and turned to leave.

"He's not in any trouble, is he?" she questioned, reading Robert's name on the card.

"Let's hope not," Robert replied as he left, shutting the door behind him. Isobel's anxiety took hold of her, and she took deep breaths, as she had been taught in her relaxation classes; in and out, in and out. Using the office phone, she tried to call Trevor on his mobile, but it went straight to voicemail.

She cancelled the call and dialled the only number she knew that would put her mind at rest. "Emergency Service, which Service do you require?"

Rosemary had left Charlotte's twenty minutes before Robert Fox called her mobile.

Sitting in the Old Plough Inn, she answered his call.

"Hi, Robert."

"Rose. Anything further to report?"

"Charlotte told me about Derek but didn't know about Jayne or Abigail. The barman here at the local pub has told me where to find Abigail, so I'm going to call in at her address. How did you get on with Trevor Johnson?" she asked.

"I was just too late, Rose, looks like someone met with him just before I arrived," he told her, sitting in his car outside of Number 14. "There was a bit of a struggle apparently, according to Isobel the Receptionist. It will no doubt be recorded on their CCTV. I've checked the dash cam that recorded the registration plate of the Range Rover which Trevor got into, and it also recorded the face of the front seat passenger."

"You were that close, Robert?" Rosemary interjected.

"We're talking minutes. I quickly checked him out. His house is seven miles away from your present location. He's married. I've texted you, his address."

"I'm on to it. Do you know who they were, Robert?"

"No, but I know a man who does. Call you soon. Signing off." The phone went dead.

****

The driver in the black cab which was parked at the end of Hays Mews continued to watch as the Ford Galaxy pulled away from outside Number Fourteen.

His mobile rang, and he listened to the caller. "Just intercepted a call to the police from Isobel Taylor. She says that she is the receptionist at Number Fourteen. We've given her the usual response and she's happy for now. The Receptionist has divulged that a female by the name of Kim Selby and our old friend, Mr Fox, has been asking for Trevor Johnson."

"Just seen him leave, Boss. Fox is on his own. Mr Johnson, however, set off with the woman, presumably Kim Selby, and others in a black Range Rover. Under duress, I'd say," the taxi driver replied.

"Bit of a coincidence that Trevor is so popular all of a sudden," the caller responded. "Stay put and get your hands on their CCTV recording."

Chapter 4

Rosemary left a voicemail message on Mrs Johnson's mobile and home telephone to contact her regarding her husband as soon as possible, as she parked outside of Abigail's house.

The detached property was an Edwardian style building set back from the road, behind a well-tendered garden and gravel drive. Abigail greeted Rosemary at the door, dressed in baggy blue dungarees and a crisp white blouse.

"So, you're looking for my father, as I have for many years," said Abigail as she led Rosemary into her lounge. "I continue to ask why my father suddenly disappeared, as did many of his belongings," Abigail said. "I have been searching high and low, but this is all I have to show for it if it helps you." Abigail took a box file from the table in front of her, opened the lid revealing an old diary from amongst newspaper clippings and other trinkets. "When the school was sold off for redevelopment, several mementoes were kept and given to the Plumpton Historic Society when I became Chair of the Society in 1998, and it is still running today. These are just some of them." Abigail passed the book to Rosemary, who traced her finger over the date with her index finger; 1968. She opened the book at the back first and read the neat italic writing in the top corner of the inside back cover. 'The Plumpton Boys'.

"Do you know what this means?" Rosemary asked Abigail, turning the inside cover of the diary to face Abigail, pointing at the entry in black ink.

"No idea," replied Abigail, dismissing the question. Rosemary committed the scribble to memory, then flicked through the pages of the diary, whilst Abigail recounted her past to her, stopping at a slight bump on one of the pages. She quickly looked down to see a page torn from the diary, committing the missing page and the date inscribed on the others to memory. Remembering what Charlotte had said, the missing page was the date when Peter Dennett had gone missing.

"Would you like to see the other mementoes of the school, Rosemary?"

Rosemary's phone vibrated in her jacket pocket. She took the phone from her pocket and recognised the number displayed on the screen.

"Sorry. Do you mind if I take this first, Abigail?"

"No, please do. Then find me in the back room. There is so much to see," Abigail replied as she rose from the settee. She left Rosemary alone in the room, turning left towards the rear of the house, as Rosemary accepted the call.

"Hi, Rosemary Bennett here."

"Hello, Miss Bennett, my name is Louise Johnson. I'm phoning about Trevor. You said it was urgent?"

"Hello, Louise. Yes, thanks for calling me back. Has Trevor been in touch with you? He wasn't at the office when my colleague called on him this afternoon."

"That is not unusual, he often has impromptu meetings in the afternoons. I probably won't see him 'till he gets home at around six this evening. Do you work with Trevor? He hasn't mentioned your name before."

"No, Louise, I don't. However, my colleague Robert called for him this morning. We'd like to speak to him about his old school days. He was whisked off in a hurry, by all accounts, and his receptionist was unable to get hold of him. Can we meet up?"

"Today?" Louise sounded concerned.

"Yes, the sooner, the better."

Rosemary sensed Louise's hesitation on the phone and added, "Miss Embling spoke very fondly of Trevor earlier today. I would really like to meet you, too."

Louise's voice changed to one of surprise, "You've seen his teacher? Trevor and I were talking about her just last night. Trevor told me that she was his favourite teacher in Primary School."

"Then let us all meet, say, at two o'clock at your house?" replied Rosemary, pinning Louise down to a time and place.

"Okay," replied Louise.

Rosemary repeated the address that Louise gave her, checking it against the one Robert had texted to her earlier, then she heard the loud chimes of a doorbell over the phone.

"Someone is at the door, must dash. Look forward to meeting you," said Louise hurriedly, and the phone line went dead.

Abigail scurried to the back room, having heard Rosemary on the phone.

Rosemary checked the phone to confirm that the connection was cut, placed the phone in her pocket and walked from the lounge through the corridor towards the back of the house. There were sounds of excited children chatting and laughing coming from the room to her left. She pushed the door open and gazed into the dimly lit, musty smelling room. There was only Abigail sitting in a chair behind an antique writing desk, at the back of the room, her head buried in a scrapbook photo album. Rosemary scanned the room, then realised that the children's voices came from a tape machine in front of the desk.

On either side of the writing desk stood a 'clothes stand', one with a black academic gown and a graduation mortarboard, on the other hung a boy's and girl's school uniform. Her eyes followed the shadows each clothes stand cast, from the bright desk lamp, along the walls which were adorned with picture frames. Rosemary could just make out some of the photos, which included a church, railway crossing gates, several of them of school classrooms, children, adults, a map of Plumpton Racecourse, and a map of the village of Plumpton Green.

In front of Rosemary, as she stepped across the threshold into the room, were two pairs of traditional school desks and chairs, which were positioned facing front, replicating the layout of an old school classroom. She stopped beside the school desks, running her fingertips over the wooden hinged lid, and then traced along the groove at the back until her fingers found the inkwell hole.

Her eyes re-focused on where Abigail was sitting and then behind her, she saw, in chalk italic writing on the blackboard, the names top to bottom of the five boys that Charlotte had reeled off earlier; John Branning, Keith Wilton, Alan Field, Trevor Johnson and lastly with his name crossed through, Derek Sargeant.

Why has she got the names on the board? Rosemary thought, looking at Abigail, *Is this a daughter's obsession about her father, or something more?*

Abigail raised her head, staring directly back at Rosemary and grinned wickedly as if she was reading Rosemary's thoughts.

Rosemary joined Abigail at the desk.

"This is my father's collection of photos that were hidden in amongst his things. So many memories," observed Abigail, as she turned another page.

"Are there any photos of you in the album?" Rosemary asked.

"I wasn't born until after my father's disappearance, unfortunately. I would have loved to have met him. He was the school's saviour; I've been told by the elders in the village. He really cared about his children."

"Do you have any children, Abigail?"

Abigail hesitated, looking down at the school children's photos in the album.

"I did once, but I lost her."

"I'm sorry," replied Rosemary.

There was an awkward silence between them.

Abigail turned the page to reveal a wide angle shot of a barn in the centre of a ploughed field.

Rosemary eyes widened having seen the photo and took the opportunity to change the subject.

"Do you know anything about the spacemen?" Rosemary asked as she pointed to the next photo taken of figures standing in front of open barn doors, all dressed in hooded all-in-one suits, with what looked like backpacks on.

"Spacemen? No," replied Abigail. "Why do you ask?"

"Just something I heard," replied Rosemary.

Charlotte had spoken to Rosemary earlier about 'the spacemen'. She had told her that the boys always talked about and drew pictures in class of the spacemen. She always thought it was their imaginations running away with them.

Rosemary refocused on the photo again, before Abigail turned the page, and just caught a glimpse of a photo of a muscle-bound young man standing in the middle of an orchard with a woman sitting on his shoulders, before Abigail slammed the album shut.

"Wasn't that your father, in the photo?" Rosemary asked.

Abigail swung her head around to face her, her stare bore into Rosemary like a laser beam points at its target.

"I must ask you to leave now, if you don't mind," said Abigail, curtly. "I have an appointment that I can't miss."

"Of course," Rosemary replied, "I've taken more than enough of your time. Hopefully, we can meet again if that's okay?"

Abigail led her to the front door, Rosemary turning on the doorstep to face her.

"I just need to ask one more question. Why do you keep all of these memorabilia?" asked Rosemary.

"It is the only real connection I have with my father's past," replied Abigail.

The door slammed shut in Rosemary's face.

Rosemary stood glaring at the door, wanting to tear it from its hinges, but thought better of it. *Not a woman to be crossed,* Rosemary thought, walking to her car in the driveway.

Pulling away from the kerb in her second-hand Toyota Yaris, she drove through the village, taking in buildings that she had seen in the framed photos hanging on the wall. She stopped outside of the convenience store, located in the centre of the village, then the row of terraced houses where the school had once stood, imagining the children at play.

Keeping a safe distance behind was a black leather-clad rider on a powerful motorbike, watching her every move.

Chapter 5

The hot sun was beating down on the outstretched parasols in the Ivy Chelsea Garden as Robert sipped his rum and coke. With his back to the old flint wall which surrounded the garden, he watched the waiting staff busying themselves around the tables, bringing food, sparkling water, and bottles of champagne to the restaurant's patrons, whilst he waited patiently for his guest to arrive.

The young girl in the floral dress brought the tall, familiar man to his table.

"Thanks for coming, Andrew."

"Always have time for you, Mr Fox," Andrew replied.

They both sat at the table facing each other.

"A drink for you, sir?" asked the girl.

"I'll have whatever he's having and get him another would you please?" replied Andrew. She nodded and left them alone at the table.

"Have you got yourself some sun, Robert? Better complexion since we last met, I notice."

"A more stress-free life now, Andrew, more of an outdoor life on the coast, all that fresh sea air. I've given up smoking, I'm saving a fortune and I generally feel so much fitter now."

"I'm still on forty a day, which is costing me a fortune. I also failed my medical and fitness test at Fort Moncton last week, so I've been told to shape up."

"Are you still a field officer?" enquired Robert, "Don't tell me that they haven't put you behind a desk yet?"

"Robert, there is no chance of me getting behind a desk. I have a line manager who is younger than my son, and his manager is younger than him. What do they want with a forty-nine-year-old foot soldier, who has spent his whole life in the Service, has trouble using the computer, and who calls a spade, a spade? I think that they are eager for me to resign. It's certainly better for them in the long run as I rattle a few cages in the Service now. They are in the habit of making too many mistakes because the senior civil servants and politicians don't learn from past ops. They'd rather pension me off, I believe," Andrew said, frustratingly to Robert, "however, they still want me to head up their covert ops on home soil."

"You have the experience on the ground which these youngsters desperately need."

"You think so. Let me tell you, Robert, it has all changed. Technology is foremost in surveillance and counter-surveillance techniques now. Budgets are being squeezed tighter every year, and therefore fewer agents are required, that means good old footwork training is not high on their agenda" – Andrew paused whilst the drinks were placed on the table, then said – "Fish for you, Robert?"

Robert nodded in agreement, "Fish and chips for us both, please."

"Very good sir", came the reply, and again they were left alone.

"Trust me when I say that you cannot beat good old-fashioned surveillance training. Your man, fresh out of nappies, so to speak, in the black cab, this morning was bloody useless. I parked up around the corner in Chesterfield Hill after my first visit to Number Fourteen, waited until Isobel, the Receptionist went for lunch, paid a couple of lads, who were up to no good, twenty quid each, to distract your man by skateboarding up to the front of his car and banging on the cab's bonnet, much to his annoyance, whilst I slipped back into Trevor Johnson's office. I showed some ID to the young man covering for Isobel, giving him the story that the CCTV had been faulty, which he accepted without question, and I replaced the CCTV recording from this morning's events with a clean tape which was placed in the storage rack above. These firms who hold all this data don't secure it at all, Andrew. You should retire and provide such a service; you'd be good at it."

Robert slid his phone over the table. "I have the original disk, Andrew, which incidentally is for the last seven days, and it shows Johnson was definitely abducted," he said in a low voice. "What I'd like to know is by whom and if you know, why?"

Andrew tapped the screen on the phone and watched the footage. He smiled, recognising the female face smiling into the CCTV camera, placed the phone back on the table, face down, and slid it back to Robert.

Robert took the phone and placed it in his pocket just as the waiter returned with the food, served them another round of drinks, then left them alone again.

"Rachel Stevens, who you can see on the CCTV, heads up a small private extraction team regularly employed by the large multinationals, to arrange for the release of captives from kidnappers abroad in places like Iraq, Afghanistan, Kuwait, and closer to home in places like Russia, but seldom in the UK. Somebody has paid her a lot of money to work here, this isn't her usual work, although her method of extraction is, the syringe needle on the side of the neck injects a muscle suppressant into the captive so they can control them in hostile situations. Rachel also works for us and SIS on odd occasions. She's a loose cannon but has a reputation for getting the job done."

"Do you trust her?"

"I tolerate her; she has her uses, Robert. As to why Trevor has been snatched is not yet apparent, however, the word is out that he has been playing around with some of his wealthy clients' mistresses, and I would suggest that one of them has taken a dislike to his antics. I'd also suggest that no real harm will come to him; Rachel wouldn't want that on her own turf and God help anyone that does. Let me warn you now, no one fucks with Rachel."

"Your man was watching the premises, Andrew. Why is 'Five' so interested in Trevor Johnson?"

"I should be asking you the same question, Robert. I shall let you go first as you invited me here today."

"Okay," replied Robert. "Trevor Johnson was one of the pupils at Plumpton Primary School in 1968 when the headmaster suddenly disappeared, and we'd like to see if he can shed any light on what happened to him. The headmaster's daughter suspects that he's still alive, and so does the sister of one of the boys, so we've been engaged to find out."

"Grasping at straws a bit, aren't you, Robert? In 1968, Trevor Johnson was just a kid."

"He was eight. You would be amazed what an adult remembers when they were a child. As you are aware, what happened to you when you were young, pleasant, or otherwise, can mould you into the adult you are today."

"Yes, indeed," affirmed Andrew, "When I was eight, all I remember is my father beating the shit out of me and my mother when he came home from the pub. That's one of the reasons I chose a university far from my hometown, to escape the daily abuse."

"Yes sorry, I remember you telling me, Andrew, but look at all of the great things you do for your son, you can't do enough for your Graham."

"Proud Dad, I am Robert. He's at Cambridge now, studying politics."

"A future Prime Minister in our midst, Andrew."

"At the moment, his attention is on females rather than politics."

"No harm in that, Andrew, he's just like his dad was when he was young."

Andrew nodded and laughed out loud, "You and me both, Robert."

"So tell me, why is 'Five' so interested in Trevor Johnson?" asked Robert, changing the subject.

"Mr Johnson's accountancy practice has been on our radar for six months now. He came to our attention when we found out that he personally prepares the management and financial accounts for a little-known test and research centre, set up on an old farm just outside of Bath. Not unusual, you might say, and it seems quite an innocuous set-up to outsiders, except that it is run by a young Chinese virologist called Tu Skreen Lee. He claims his team of scientists have developed a new vaccine, which can combat the SARS coronavirus in humans and may also help stem the spread of other mutated viruses such as HIV, swine flu and bird flu.

"To date, there has never been a breakthrough for severe acute respiratory syndrome; they state that research is ongoing, but if this research centre's claims are true, then the Royal Society of Pathology wants to announce the vaccine first, as being developed in the UK. Even more important to our scientists at Public Health England, or PHE as they are widely known as, and the World Health Organisation, is how this vaccine has been developed and is not being notified to them. In the past, both health organisations were aware, and fully up to speed, when SARS was contracted in China in 2002, where it is thought that a strain of the coronavirus, usually only found in mammals, mutated, enabling it to affect humans. Back then, eight thousand people were infected, of which ten percent died, mainly aged sixty-five and over. We were lucky in the UK that only four of its population died, but that was down to a successful campaign to isolate those with pneumonia at hospitals around the country, to stop further spread."

"So where does Trevor fit into this, Andrew?" Robert asked, fully aware of the far wider implication of meeting with Mr Trevor Johnson.

"He knows that we have sufficient evidence on his afternoon playtime activities to discredit him and his business. Being a successful accountant relies on trust, so if you found out that your accountant is bedding your wife, or discussing pillow talk about your private business dealings with your mistress, you would want serious payback."

"So, you persuaded him to work for you?"

"To be our informant, Robert. You know how this works, and for his Intel, we suppress any information about his antics, and he retains his credibility and his marriage intact to his loving wife."

Chapter 6

Trevor Johnson and his wife reside in one of the largest houses on Dyke Road Avenue, just northwest of Brighton town centre.

Beautiful homes, Rosemary thought to herself, admiring the large, detached houses set back from the highway, behind high boundary walls and tall wrought-iron gates.

She spotted the open gates of the Johnson's residence on her right, and steered the car into the driveway, and stopped outside of the front door of the impressive two-storey mock Tudor house.

Rosemary saw the front door ajar and sensed that something wasn't right.

Rosemary stepped out of the car and gingerly walked up to the front door. Rosemary listened intently through the gap in the door, but all she could hear was a slow soft ticking from the other side of the door. *Perhaps from a grandfather clock*, she thought. She gently pushed the door open with her elbow, the bright sunshine cast her shadow across the wooden parquet flooring in the hallway, leading to a wide-sweeping carpeted staircase that led to the first floor.

"Hello. Mrs Johnson?"

There was no answer, just the perpetual Tick-Tock of a clock. She stepped inside, glancing first right and then left. The hallway was enormous, the glazed balustrade staircase the main feature, leading to the landing that swept left and right. She looked up and behind her, above the front door, to see shutters closed over the large arched window and the steep pitch of the skeiling to the ridge of the roof above.

"Hello", she called out again, but still no answer. Just the soft ticking of the large grandfather clock she spotted, standing between two sets of gloss white double doors that were closed shut within their ornately sculptured architraves. She stepped back over the threshold of the door, being careful not to touch the door or frame, and turned towards the car to see a woman striding into the driveway.

A tall, elegant woman dressed in a floral dress looked at Rosemary and then the open front door.

"Oh my god!" she exclaimed, raising her left hand to her forehead.

"Don't tell me I left the door unlocked again!"

"Mrs Johnson?" Rosemary enquired.

"Yes."

"Hello. I'm Rosemary. I found the door ajar when I arrived."

"You're five minutes early. I was expecting you to arrive at two. I raced around to my neighbour to get some milk because I had run out." She held up the plastic bottle of milk in her right hand to confirm her story. "I saw the car turn into the drive from Tracey's next door. I couldn't have closed the door properly. Can you believe my stupidity?" She reached the front door and smiled at Rosemary, as she passed her by. "Come in and I shall put the kettle on."

Rosemary followed.

Louise stepped over the threshold. "Alexa, open shutter," she commanded.

There was a soft hum of an electric motor, which powered the wooden shutters open, allowing the bright sunlight to fill the hallway, through the large arched window above the door.

Rosemary admired the blush-coloured hallway walls adorned with large paintings set into gilt frames. Pride of place at the top of the stairs was a full-size painting of Trevor in top hat and tailcoat and his wife in her wedding dress, standing in the archway of a church, which Rosemary recognised instantly.

"Were you were married at St Laurence Church in Telscombe Village, Mrs Johnson?" she queried.

"Yes, we were," replied Mrs Johnson as she opened a door to her right.

"It's my favourite church," Rosemary responded, thinking back to her earlier visits to the 10th Century parish sanctuary.

"Come in, make yourself at home." She showed Rosemary through to the spacious Edwardian Conservatory which looked out onto a well-tendered garden.

Rosemary yearned for a garden where the grass was cut short and rolled flat like a bowling green, with an array of a blossoming cottage garden and bedding plants, which had been carefully positioned in the external beds. She eyed the garden with envy. *I live in a flat in Brighton with empty flower boxes on the balcony that used to face the sea*, she thought, *and all I see now is reflective glass panels of the apartment block across the road.*

"I met Charlotte Embling recently," Rosemary started the conversation, wanting to keep Charlotte's married name to herself. "She tells me that she was Trevor's teacher when he joined the school just after his fifth birthday and remained so until he was eight."

"That's right. He and his friends were really upset when she left. Trevor hadn't seen her since then, not until yesterday when he told me that he met her in Selfridges when he was buying me this vase," Louise pointed at the white lilies in the tall crystal cut vase on the windowsill. "Trevor always buys me white lilies for my birthday."

"Is it your birthday today, Louise?" enquired Rosemary.

"Yes," Louise replied in excitement, "and I'm looking forward to Trevor getting home. He is taking me to Edinburgh tonight to spend the weekend with my parents. I haven't seen them for months, so we are flying from Gatwick tonight."

"Happy Birthday," Rosemary responded, "I shall keep this brief then Louise," Rosemary said, as she plucked the school photo from her bag, placing it on the table in front of Louise.

Louise looked down at the photo, a smile beamed across her face and pointing to Trevor said, "What a coincidence, we have a copy of this photo in Trevor's album. He was showing it to me last night."

"Can I see it?" Rosemary asked.

Louise left the room for just a moment and returned with a sepia coloured scrapbook photo album, similar to Abigail Wilton's. She opened the album to reveal a headshot of Trevor when he was eight years of age, and underneath, in chalk italic writing, was his name, Trevor Johnson.

"He still has that cheeky grin," Louise replied.

"How long have you been married?" asked Rosemary.

"It will be twenty-nine years this August," replied Louise proudly, "he is so good to me and I don't know what I'd do without him."

Rosemary decided not to bring up the subject of him being whisked away from his office.

"I thought that he would have tired of me and left me long ago, especially when we found out that I couldn't have children. He would be a great father."

Rosemary could sense the disappointment in Louise's voice.

"Was adoption not an option?" she asked.

"Not for Trevor. He could not accept raising someone else's child. We have fun with Katie and Will, my sister's children when we have them stay some weekends. Trevor always says he loves to spend time with them, but then he adds that it's always nice to be able to give them back, and I agree with him, because we have little time to ourselves, when he's not at work."

Louise turned to the next page and the next to reveal Trevor, first as a baby and then at each birthday thereafter.

"His father and mother put the album together of his life, and we have since added our photos to it." She turned the page to see a monotone photo of a woman in shorts and a tight-fitting top sitting on a man's shoulders. The man and woman were laughing at the camera, the man holding the woman tight around her thighs, as she was reaching up for a ball, which was stuck in the branches of an apple tree. *The same photo as she had seen at Abigail's house,* she thought.

"Who is the woman atop the young man's shoulders?" Rosemary asked.

"Trevor's mother, Teresa," replied Louise, pointing at the woman. "Trevor always seems angry when he turns to this page and he skips over it, quickly and without comment, whenever we reminisce about each of our albums. I did ask him if he knew the man, but Trevor just says that he was somebody that his parents knew. Trevor is a very quiet man who seldom loses his temper, but whenever I mention or ask him about the man in the photo, he becomes reclusive hiding himself away in his shed at the top of the garden. I haven't mentioned it for over a year now and am wondering whether to remove the photo, to be honest."

Rosemary identified the man in the picture.

"Do you recognise him?" asked Louise.

"His name is Peter Dennett."

"Do you think that this man has done something to hurt Trevor?"

"I don't know if he has done anything wrong, but I do know that Peter Dennett was the Headmaster of Plumpton Primary School at the time when Trevor was at school there, Louise" – replied Rosemary and added – "Peter Dennett went missing when Trevor was eight. I was hoping that Trevor and his classmates would be able to help me find out why he went missing."

"From the reaction that Trevor has to this photo, I would say that he wasn't a fan of this man," Louise replied, turning the photo to face Rosemary, watching carefully for any reaction.

"Peter Dennett, by all accounts, was well respected by the children and parents alike, Louise. He was the school's saviour, apparently, and if it wasn't for him, then there would have been no school in Plumpton. He had Miss Embling's full admiration, so it seems."

"Then why can't Trevor say his name, or talk about him?"

"You need to ask Trevor that," Rosemary replied.

Louise was about to say something when the doorbell chimed. She sprung up out of her seat and stormed out of the conservatory towards the front door.

The room fell quiet, and Rosemary listened to Louise's shoe-clip along the parquet wooden floor to the front door, then a cheery woman's voice.

"Hello. Mrs Johnson, Mrs Trevor Johnson?"

"Yes, that's me."

"Happy Birthday Mrs Johnson. Have a nice day."

She heard the door close shut, and footsteps coming back towards the conservatory.

Louise sat down beside Rosemary again, placed the brown paper package on the table in front of them, then, turning to Rosemary, asked, "Why are you so intent on finding Trevor's headmaster?"

"He may have more information on how Derek Sargeant died."

"What more information can he have? Trevor told me that he and his friends were with Derek when he died. In fact, he died in his teacher's arms. He said that it was a very sad day for all of them at school. He remembers that he was told it was a heart attack that killed him and that nobody knew that he had a heart condition, not even his mother. God bless her."

"It must have been very painful for her," Rosemary replied.

"What did the headmaster do to help Derek?" asked Louise.

"He didn't do anything, he couldn't, because he wasn't at the school that day, Louise, he was reported missing on the day Derek died."

"Why then does Trevor react in such a way when he sees this photo?" asked Louise.

"I don't know, you may find that only Trevor can tell you why?"

"Perhaps he'll tell you. Would you stay please, until he gets home? He shouldn't be long now, he's usually here by six."

Rosemary checked her watch. Five-thirty.

"Okay, I shall stay and ask him, no promises though."

"Thanks. I'll make us some coffee and a bite to eat, and then I'll show you my birthday surprise," Louise replied, then left Rosemary alone in the conservatory.

"I shall just catch up on my messages," Rosemary called out to Louise, as she watched her skip out of the conservatory. She craned her neck to read the message on the brown package resting on the table. It read, *Mrs Johnson – For Your Eyes Only*.

She grabbed her phone out of her inside jacket pocket and listened to the only message received. "Rose, Trevor has been caught with his pants down with a mistress of one of his clients. The client arranged an extraction team to snatch him this morning, then frightened him a bit, persuaded him to keep his mouth shut, and then let him go. The client is livid and wanted to teach him a lesson and send everyone else a message not to mess with him. Trevor is a little bit battered and bruised, but otherwise okay. He's on his way home. Hope everything is okay, your end. Signing off."

She typed her reply, 'Thanks for the message, Robert, I'm fine and at Louise's house. Good to hear that Trevor's on his way home. Been persuaded to stay. I shall tell Louise Johnson that he should be home soon. See you tonight at the Marina,' and pushed send.

She slipped her phone back into her pocket just as Louise returned, carrying a silver tray laden with scones adorned with jam and cream and a pot of tea.

Louise eyed the package with excitement.

"Trevor spoils me so much on my birthday," she said, picking up the package, removing the sticky tape from the neatly folded end, her beaming smile showing off her bright white teeth.

She peered inside to see a wodge of photographs. She tipped the brown packaging up on its end and let the contents spill out onto the table.

Both women stared at the photos; horror etched on their faces at the sordid images of Trevor naked on a bed with two naked Asian women.

"What the hell!" screamed Louise, transfixed by the scenes before her, scattered across the table. "No!" came the guttural cry as she spread her hands across the table, trying in vain to gather the photos together so that she could hide the images out of sight from her guest.

Rosemary stood from her seat, and stretching her hands out over the table, helped Louise to collect the photos, turning them over as she did so, to hide the images. Louise snatched the photos from Rosemary's hands, clutching them to her body, then picking up the packaging, stormed out of the open conservatory doors into the garden, towards an incinerator, where she cast them into the metal bin.

Rosemary saw Louise staring into the incinerator, then turned, and with her head held high, Louise walked calmly back to where Rosemary was sitting in silence, watching her every move.

"I would like you to leave, now please," she said, as tears started to run down her face, causing her eyeliner to smudge and run down her once-perfect makeup. "I want to be alone."

Without another word, Louise paced quickly toward the front door, with Rosemary following closely behind. Rosemary turned to face Louise before stepping over the threshold. "Will you…?"

"I will be fine," Louise replied sharply, her expression becoming stoic, and she slammed the door behind her.

Rosemary stood on the mat outside of the front door, listening in silence. First, there was nothing, then she saw the curtains being closed in the front rooms, one by one, and then silence.

****

The lone motorcycle leather-clad figure, hidden in the bushes at the front of the house, smiled to herself, having witnessed the front door slam, and watched as the car turned out of the gate. "Now let the fun begin, Trevor."

Chapter 7

Rosemary awoke to the sound of a door closing, then she smelt the aroma of toast and coffee wafting into her bedroom through the partially opened door. She threw the duvet off her, swung her legs out of bed, and looked at her fully clothed body in the long mirror next to the wardrobe, then back at the bed.

"That's not the duvet I had on the bed last night," she muttered to herself.

She ran her fingers through her hair twice, then slowly shuffled her way out of her bedroom towards the kitchen door, grabbing the glass paper weight from the hallway table. Holding the paperweight high above her head, she quietly crept towards the kitchen door, stopping momentarily when she heard the radio playing classical music quietly from the kitchen.

She opened the kitchen-diner door to see Robert placing boiled eggs in their cups on the table and covering them with her favourite knitted bunny cosies.

"Good morning, Rose. You're awake. Breakfast is ready for you on the table," he said cheerily, as he pulled the chair out from under the table for her to sit on.

"Robert! What are you doing in my flat?" she asked, as she lowered the paper weight in her hand, behind her back.

"You gave me a key, remember? When you didn't turn up last night, I came round to check that you were okay, and when I arrived, you were crashed out on top of the bed, so I covered you over with the spare duvet, and made myself comfortable on the settee for the night."

Rosemary looked at the settee to see that it was clear of the papers that she had been reading a couple of days ago, the pillows which she had thrown on the floor were now neatly positioned, across the seat.

"Sorry, Robert. I stood you up again."

"You did." He nodded and raised his eyebrows at her in mock admonishment.

She was genuinely hurt because this was the third time she had failed to meet up with him. "I must admit, I was exhausted after the day's events with Charlotte and Louise yesterday; I'm truly sorry Robert, I must be your worst BFF." She ran her fingers through her hair again, in an effort to look half-decent.

"BFF?"

"Best Friend Forever." She laughed, sat down next to him, placing the paper weight on the table, and pecked him on his cheek. He turned and smiled.

"You can tell me all about what happened yesterday, later. Eat up, we are off somewhere together today."

"Today? It's Saturday, Robert. I was planning on doing some shopping. I have no food in the house."

"I noticed."

She looked at the two boiled eggs, a rack of toast, orange juice, and croissants in front of her. "You've been shopping, Robert," she commented. She looked around at the sparkling clean kitchen worktops, to see that they were clear of two days' worth of dirty plates, pots, and pans.

"You've washed up my mess as well. You'll be ironing my knickers next!" she sniggered, then tucked into her breakfast.

"No, I left them on the floor where you dropped them." He watched her mouth gape open at his comment and he burst into laughter.

"It's no laughing matter, Robert," Rosemary remarked, "I don't want you getting the wrong idea," to which he laughed even louder. "I mean it, Robert. I'm not usually so slovenly."

"I know what you mean", he responded, with a cheeky grin.

Rosemary smiled. "Thanks for the breakfast, Robert." She looked at the man who had walked into her office just over a year ago. She had instantly warmed to him and now, well now, he was her perfect business partner and wondered if he felt any affection towards her.

"You said we are going somewhere today, Robert, doing what exactly?"

"Finish your breakfast and get yourself ready, Rose, I thought we would take a trip out, rather than you and me both sitting alone for the weekend."

"Perhaps we can have lunch out as well. I'll pay," replied Rosemary.

"I've already prepared lunch as it's such a sunny day, Rose. I hope you like picnics?" he asked as he showed her the packed hamper.

"Wow!" She saw the Fortnum and Mason hamper motif on the front of the wicker basket, filled to the top with food placed in amongst the straw packing.

She gulped down the last morsels of food, jumped up from the chair and cheerfully said, "I shall be just a few minutes, Robert."

She skipped towards the door, spun around and with a beaming smile, said, "Thanks, Robert," before disappearing out of sight.

Just under 30 minutes later, Robert looked up slowly from the morning Times newspaper to see Rosemary standing at the door.

Robert feast his eyes first on Rosemary's bright white trainers, her slim calves below her daisy midi skirt, a touch of bare midriff and her white blouse tied around her waist. He was a silent fan of the slight curls of her mousey brown hair, which fell naturally around her face, and her blue eyes which radiated such warmth, her small perfectly formed nose and her smile that would brighten the dullest day.

"Will I do, Robert?" she asked.

He smiled. "You'll do," he responded.

"Thanks", Rosemary replied sarcastically, her smile disappearing in an instant.

"No, you look great. Really!"

She smiled again.

****

"Ready?" asked Robert, as he engaged the first gear of his trusty Ford Galaxy.

"Where are we going?" enquired Rosemary excitedly.

"We are heading to Chalk Hills Riding Stables, the one I told you about, at the foot of the South Downs in Southwick, just west of here. It will take all of twenty minutes to get there."

Rosemary took in the beautiful scenery on the route there, and Robert could see that she was enjoying the views, so kept silent.

He steered his Ford Galaxy into the driveway and stopped outside of the front door to the owner's home. Stepping out of the car, they both saw a young woman in her light blue top, white breeches, and long black riding boots, bounding towards them from the stables ahead of them, waving excitedly. "Hi, Robert, great to see you again."

She reached Robert in an instant and flung her arms around his neck, planting a single kiss on his cheek, then let go, and turning to Rosemary, said, "Hi."

"Rosemary, let me introduce you to Paulina," said Robert.

"Hi there," Rosemary responded, checking out the tall, slender horse rider.

"It's a lovely day to go riding on the Downs" – Paulina said as she turned towards the stables – "follow me, everything is ready."

Rosemary kept pace with Robert as they followed Paulina towards the stables.

"What have you got me into, Robert? I'm hardly dressed for horse riding," she tittered as they strode through the open stable door into the empty room.

Paulina pulled back the hessian curtain hanging against the wall to reveal two matching electric bikes in a brick alcove.

"Who said anything about horse riding?" replied Robert, watching Rosemary's reaction.

Rosemary burst into laughter. "Robert! I haven't ridden a bicycle since school. What happens if I fall off?"

"You'll get dirty," Robert responded smiling, "Paulina will be happy to show you how the electric motor works on the bike."

Pushing the bikes out of the stables, Paulina showed Rosemary how to operate the motor whilst Robert fetched the picnic basket.

He watched the two women ride around the paddock laughing with each other and smiled as he noticed how well Rosemary handled the bike. Rosemary and Paulina pulled up on either side of him.

"Shall we go?" Robert asked.

"Ready when you are," she replied excitedly.

Paulina steadied his bike whilst Robert secured the basket to the rack behind the seat, then having mounted the bike, he led the way up the track over Southwick Hill to Thunders Barrow, where they stopped. He spread out the picnic rug on the raised promontory of the South Downs and set out the food, as Rosemary took in the uninterrupted view of the coastline from Shoreham Harbour to Brighton Pier. "This spot is beautiful, Robert; how did you know about it?"

"Stewart and Marcia own The Stables and have been friends and work colleagues of mine since I joined the Service. They looked out for me when my wife died ten years ago, Stewart becoming my soulmate during my darkest days. I stayed with them for eight months, whilst I sorted my life out. They both shared my grief and convinced me that there was life outside of the Service. I left the

Service six months after my wife's funeral and started working three months after that, with Stewart in his private security business.

"It was very fortuitous that you were looking for a business partner a year ago, Rose because Stewart was considering his retirement."

Rosemary smiled. "And Paulina?"

"They couldn't have children and whilst stationed out in Poland twenty-two years ago, they took in a young girl who they found at an orphanage. She had no name, and so they raised her as their own, naming her Paulina after the nun who gave her to them. Sadly, three weeks after they took her back to their flat in Warsaw, there was a fire at the orphanage that destroyed the building and everything in it."

"And the children, Robert?"

"The story told was that all of the doors were padlocked shut from the outside and there were no survivors."

Rosemary closed her eyes tight shut, as she imagined the horror within the orphanage and a single tear ran down her cheek, which she swept away with her fingertips. "Who on earth would do something so horrific, Robert?"

"Apparently, the benefactors of the orphanage, who themselves couldn't have children, ceased funding the refuge after rumours of abuse to the children spread throughout the village, so they decided to move the children to another orphanage near Radom, a town south-east of Warsaw. The nun vehemently defended herself and others of the allegations and in a fit of rage against the village and the benefactors, she padlocked the doors and windows shut and set fire to the building. She then hung herself from the large oak tree, which grew next to the village church. In her letter found on her body, she said that if she couldn't care for her children, then no one could."

"Does Paulina know, Robert?"

"No, and she mustn't know."

"Got that," Rosemary acknowledged.

There was almost silence around them, except for the chirping of male crickets on the ground.

Rosemary sat on the picnic rug opposite Robert and toppled her head back to let the bright sun radiate its midday heat on her face. "You are full of surprises Robert, thank you for bringing me out today. It is so lovely here. Did I tell you that Trevor and Louise couldn't have children?" Rosemary asked.

Robert shook his head.

"Trevor wouldn't adopt, even though Louise craved for a child. She worshipped the ground he walked on, Robert. She showed me Trevor's scrapbook, which had photos of Trevor from when he was a baby, through his teenage years, and then skipping through the album, showed me photos of their wedding right up to their present day. She spoke so fondly of him until she found out about his infidelities. I saw the photos of him romping on the bed with two Chinese women.

"She was horrified, Robert, she asked me to leave, which I did immediately and then she proceeded to close all the curtains at the front of the house. I've been worrying about her since, poor woman."

He nodded. "Hope she's okay, Rose. Come on, eat up, we should make tracks. We shall be stopping on the route."

On their way back, Robert stopped at the Saracen stone known as 'Rest and Be Thankful' at the top of the hill, to wait for Rosemary to catch up.

He dismounted and sat on the square stone seat. Rosemary dismounted and joined him, snuggling up next to him. "This stone is known as 'Rest and Be Thankful'"

"Quite an apt name, for all who need to rest for a while," Rosemary remarked, as she stretched her legs in front of her.

"It's my favourite spot. I used to sit here for hours on end, just thinking about my wife, Jenny mainly, and greeting the walkers, horse riders, and cyclists as they went by. Some would stop and talk, and others would just pass by, without a word."

"It's a lovely spot, Robert." She turned her head towards him. "How did your wife die, Robert?"

"She was killed by a speeding motorcycle. Jenny was meeting me for lunch opposite the Royal Albert Hall when the motorbike hit with such force, the rider killed her before I even reached her. I feel that I'm responsible and so try not to talk about it, Rose."

"I'm sorry, Robert," Rosemary replied, placing her hand on his. Robert felt Rosemary's soft warm hand on his, closed his eyes and thought of Jenny. Without warning, he slid his hand from under hers and stood up quickly.

"Time to go, Rose, it's all downhill from here," he said, as he grabbed the grips on the handlebars and mounted the bike.

Rosemary could sense that she had struck a nerve with Robert, and immediately regretted asking him about his wife. She watched him as he set off down the hill and quickly followed.

Chapter 8

Rosemary closed the door to her flat, and as she leant back against it, reflected on the day she'd had with Robert.

As she walked through the corridor to the kitchen, her eye glimpsed the screen of her mobile light up, then flash three times, through the open door to the bedroom.

"I'll forget my head one day," she muttered to herself as she continued into the kitchen. She flicked the kettle on and whilst waiting for it to boil, collected her phone from the bedside table in the bedroom.

There were eight missed calls and six voicemails, all from the same number.

Rosemary listened to the first message.

"Rosemary, it's Charlotte. Please call me back as soon as you can." Charlotte's voice was brittle.

She listened to the second.

"Rosemary. It's Charlotte again. I have just had the police at my door. It's about Trevor Johnson, Rosemary. Call me back urgently please!" Now her voice sounded angry.

The remainder of the messages all demanded that she phone her back.

She looked at the bedside clock; it was just after nine in the evening. The phone rang and she instantly recognised Robert's number. She accepted the call.

"Hi, Robert."

"Rose, I have just had a call from one of my contacts. He tells me that the police are currently at the Johnson's residence. Neighbours were complaining about the loud music being played earlier today, so the local beat officers have been to investigate and have found Louise dead in her home."

"Dead? How?"

"Don't know yet, but they suspect foul play. Does anyone know that you were with Trevor's wife today, Rose?"

"The neighbour maybe. Louise was getting some milk from next door when I arrived, but that's not all. Charlotte has been leaving messages on my mobile this evening, saying that she wants to talk about Trevor. She has had the police turn up at her place and she wants me to call her back."

"Call her back, Rose. Tell her you'll be there as quickly as you can. I shall come with you to see her. We need to find out what was said. I'll make some calls on the way. See you in twenty minutes."

"Thanks, Robert."

Rosemary hung up and immediately made the next call. "Charlotte? Rosemary here. You have left several messages for me to call you."

"I've been trying to reach you all day," exclaimed Charlotte, "you didn't return my calls, and to be honest, you are not my greatest fan at the moment." Charlotte's voice was stentorian. "The last thing I need is police turning up on my doorstep, after all these years, asking me about one of my old school pupils. Have you told them where I live, Rosemary?"

"No Charlotte, I've spoken to no one."

"Then who did?"

"Good question," replied Rosemary.

"I told them everything about meeting Trevor and you visiting me, unannounced, yesterday. Why didn't you answer my calls?"

Rosemary tried to speak, but Charlotte pressed on.

"Up until yesterday, I was content being alone, and now—"

"What did?" Rosemary tried to ask what the police had said, but Charlotte bit back.

"Don't interrupt me, when I'm talking," she shouted down the phone, "If you hadn't come to see me, then I wouldn't have the police turning up at my door."

"Charlotte!" Rosemary shouted down the phone.

"What!" Charlotte replied.

Rosemary could hear her hyperventilating.

"You asked me to call you back, and I'm sorry it's so late. I left my phone by my bed when I went out, and I've only just got in. I'm sorry Charlotte. I can come round now, this minute, and we can talk about what's happened, if you want to."

Charlotte's rapid breathing subsided, then silence.

"Charlotte?" There was a silent pause.

"Yes please," she replied, "I'd appreciate some company, right now." Rosemary heard Charlotte take a deep breath and then exhale loudly. Another breath and then she continued, "I was very shocked when two Police Officers turned up at my front door."

"I shall be around in half an hour; my colleague Robert will be with me. Is that okay, Charlotte?"

"Yes, Rosemary. See you then. Thank you." Rosemary heard a doorbell ring just before Charlotte hung up.

****

The motorcycle leather-clad figure watched Charlotte emerge from her front door, turning her head left then right, searching for the unknown visitor who had rung the doorbell.

Charlotte stepped further out of the house, scanning the bushes around her bungalow.

"Hello Charlotte," the unknown figure muttered under their breath.

****

Rosemary looked at herself in the mirror. *Time for a change of clothes*, she thought.

She quickly changed into blue jeans and an army green blouse, leaving the other clothes scattered over the bed.

She left her flat and waited on the pavement outside of the street entrance door, quickly checking her reflection in the large glazing panel next to the front door.

She saw Robert turn into the street in his Ford Galaxy and crossed the road, ready to jump into his car, just as the police car pulled up outside of her entrance door.

Robert leant over and pushed the door open, "Get in, Rose."

The two policewomen took no notice of her getting into the car as they pressed the entry phone buzzer to her flat.

"That was close, Rose. Let's see what they have told Charlotte before they question you."

"What do you mean, Robert?"

"My sources tell me that Trevor has also been found dead. The police believe that they weren't alone and that the cause of their deaths is being treated as suspicious."

"Robert, just before Charlotte hung up, her doorbell rang. You don't think she's in danger, do you?"

"I hope not, Rose. We'll be there in less than ten minutes," he replied as he punched the emergency number into his phone.

****

Charlotte could sense that she was being watched. She was sure that someone had whispered her name. She stood still, holding her breath, acutely listening for a sound, but she heard nothing except her heart beating harder. She couldn't hold her breath any longer, her lungs weren't what they used to be, and she exhaled long and hard until her lungs deflated. The sudden release of air from her lungs made her feel light-headed, and as she turned to walk back to her front door, she spied out of the corner of her eye a dark figure darting inside her home. Her heart started to beat quicker, harder; Charlotte took two hurried steps, her feet slipping on the damp grass beneath her, causing her to fall backwards heavily. Her arms couldn't stop her head from hitting the ground, momentarily knocking her unconscious.

****

The full-beam headlights of the Ford Galaxy shone through the bars of Charlotte's front gate into the garden beyond, as Robert drove towards the end of the cul-de-sac.

"Oh my god, Robert, stop! It's Charlotte."

The car skidded to a halt, Rosemary flung the passenger door open and hurdled over the gate and ran towards Charlotte.

Impressive, thought Robert as he stepped from the car, leaving the engine running, so that the beams of bright white light, from the headlights, shone on the old lady lying on the ground.

"Charlotte, can you hear me?" Rosemary asked, as she stroked her head gently. "Charlotte, it's me, Rosemary. Just tell me you are okay."

Rosemary saw Charlotte's eyes open; her mouth was moving, trying to tell her something. "Stay still, help is on its way," Rosemary reassured her, seeing Robert at the open gate with his mobile to his ear in one hand and the picnic rug in the other. She knew she didn't have to ask him to call for an ambulance. He finished the call and paced over to them.

Charlotte's hand lifted off the ground, her finger pointing towards the front door. "Someone's there," she trembled.

Robert heard Charlotte too, as he laid the rug over Charlotte and pointed to the blood-stained hair on Charlotte's head.

Rosemary nodded in acknowledgement. "Check out who is in there, will you, Robert?" He nodded and started towards the front door, when another pair of bright beams from a car's headlights danced across the grass, illuminating the elevation of the bungalow, casting his shadow on to the white rendered finish, as the police car came to an abrupt stop next to the Ford Galaxy.

Rosemary recognised the two policewomen who had been at her place earlier as they disembarked from the car.

"Stop where you are," commanded the first officer, as she focused the flashlight on Robert's back.

The second officer hurried towards Rosemary and Charlotte.

"Hands on your head where I can see them and get down on your knees, now!" came the second command. Robert stood still, raised his hands, and placed them on his head, then bending his knees, sunk to the floor, facing the bungalow. The policewoman took no time in reaching him, kneed him in the back forcing him, face forward, to the ground and shouted, "hands behind your back, now!" Robert obliged, smarting at the pain in his back.

The policewoman recited the obligatory caution as she snapped the handcuffs tightly around his wrists. Robert didn't struggle, he shook his head, and warned her not to go near the bungalow, whilst she led him to the rear of the police car, guiding him into the rear seat, and closing the door.

Rosemary comforted Charlotte as she explained to the second officer who Charlotte, she and Robert were, and that an intruder was in the bungalow.

"The Robert Fox, personal friend of the DCI" exclaimed the officer, as she turned her head to see Robert's head duck into the rear of the police car.

"Yes, that's him."

"It's just not our day," she replied and turned to her colleague. Pointing towards the front door, she mouthed, "There is someone in the bungalow, watch out."

The first policewoman acknowledged her warning and cautiously made her way towards the front door, shining her high-powered torch through the opening. "It's the police," she shouted as she approached the threshold.

From the rear seat of the car, Robert saw a shapely leather motorcycle clad figure sprint into view from inside the residence, slamming into the policewoman, bowling her over onto her back, and then turning to their left, running towards the side boundary fence, bounding over it like a cat, and was gone. *Whoever that was, she was nimble and strong*, he thought, as he watched the battered and bruised policewoman pick herself up off the ground, cursing to herself whilst holding her buttocks, and grimacing in pain.

The paramedics arrived along with the Detective Chief Inspector and stood by Robert's car, waiting for the 'all clear' to proceed from the first policewoman, before moving beyond the gate.

Whilst the paramedics tended to Charlotte, the first policewoman debriefed the events to the DCI. "I've managed to detain one of the suspects, but the woman got away," she explained as she led him back to the police car, "I've alerted control and assistance is on its way."

"Are you okay, Trish?" asked the DCI.

"Yes sir, my ego is more battered and bruised than I am," she replied, smarting at the pain.

"Best get you checked out," replied the Detective Chief Inspector. "Shame she got away. She may have something to do with the two deaths on Dyke Road Avenue."

"At the Johnson's place, Sir? We were told it was a suicide pact."

"It was made to look like that, but SOCO has found evidence that Trevor and Louise Johnson were both murdered; it isn't common knowledge, Trish, so keep it under your hat."

"Of course sir, but at least we have a suspect."

The Detective Chief Inspector leaned forward to see the detainee in the car and opened the rear door. "What have you been getting yourself into, Robert?" he asked, as he motioned Robert to step out of the car. "Release him, Constable Berry. This is my old colleague, Robert Fox."

"You're Robert Fox?"

Robert nodded.

"The man who solved the poisoning case at Brighton University," she responded, as she removed the cuffs from Robert, who nodded in appreciation. "I'm going to be the laughingstock of the station."

"What you did was textbook stuff," Robert commended, "well done, Constable."

"Thank you, Sir, I'm sorry I let the real suspect get away."

"It's okay. Happens to me all the time."

"Yeah, right," she replied and walked away, shaking her head.

"It's been a long time Robert," said the DCI, shaking Robert's hand.

"It certainly has Peter, thanks for coming," replied Robert. "Is your constable going to be okay?"

"She'll be ribbed for nicking you for a few weeks, but after that, it will be forgotten."

"I heard you say that the Johnsons are dead."

"You didn't hear it from me, Robert, but it looks like they weren't the only ones in their house yesterday."

They both watched Rosemary comforting the elderly woman as she was stretchered into the ambulance. "Who's with you, Robert?"

"Rose Bennett. She's a good one, Peter. We've both been working on the missing headmaster case that I briefed you about."

"And where does the elderly woman and the Johnson's factor into this?"

"Charlotte was a teacher and Trevor Johnson was a pupil at the same school at the time Peter Dennett, the headmaster, disappeared."

"You think that the deaths of the Johnson's and what happened here are linked?"

"I do now."

"Did you see the assailant escape, Robert?"

"Yes Peter, I'm sure that it was a woman and a strong and agile one at that, but Trish will confirm my suspicions. Finding this missing Headmaster is proving more complicated than first thought, and I'm trying to figure out where the woman in leathers jigsaws into this puzzle."

****

The leather motorcycle clad woman was in such a rage, she hadn't checked her speed as she gunned the Yamaha into the coastal town of Peacehaven, the speed camera flashing twice recording the motorbike's number plate; the roar of the engine drowning out her scream of anger.

Through gritted teeth, she promised to herself, "You will all pay!"

Chapter 9

The lone figure was on the edge of the seat of the settee, staring at the newsfeed on the News at ten, describing the international concern raised about the Ebola outbreak in the Republic of the Congo. He knew that his research should have gone public for the good of mankind, but there was a major flaw in what should have been the life-saving drug of the century.

Alan Manville's research with Tu Skreen Lee on a vaccine for SARS had stumbled upon a possible vaccine for Ebola too, but news about the scientific development had not hit the headlines and probably never would. During the trials on the various animals, the agent resembling the disease-causing microorganism had mutated in the lab during trials and had resulted in the death of the entire bat colony, at the research centre in Timsbury, a small hamlet just outside of Bath.

He couldn't understand what had gone so badly wrong. Everything was perfect, or so it seemed.

He had become disillusioned over the last year about the true intentions of Tu Skreen Lee; Lee knew that the vaccine was flawed and yet he had falsified the data, before he sent it in June 2019, to the research centre in Wuhan, China, where trials on humans were about to begin.

It had been just over a month since he blurted out his concerns, over a private dinner in the Ivy Brasserie, in Bath, to his school friend and Tu Skreen Lee's accountant, Trevor Johnson.

Alan fumbled around the settee for the remote control to switch off the TV, just as he caught a glimpse of the wedding photo of Trevor and his wife Louise which filled the screen; the subtitles below reading "Brighton couple murdered".

He paused and focused on the newsfeed, to see the reporter standing outside of Trevor's home, in front of the police taped off cordon.

He perched even closer on the edge of the settee and listened intently to the female reporter as she delivered the latest news.

"Thank you, Clive. I'm standing outside of the property, in the usually quiet and salubrious district of Brighton and Hove, where Police have found the bodies of Trevor and Louise Johnson."

The camera panned away from the reporter and focused on the open front door of the house, where people in white overalls and blue overshoes were exiting the building, carrying full black plastic bags.

The camera then panned back towards the reporter, skimming over the array of Police vehicles parked within and around the cordon. The focus of the lens was now directly on the female reporter.

"It was initially thought, when the bodies were found this morning, that this was a double suicide. However, there is mounting evidence, which suggests that both Mr and Mrs Johnson have been murdered. Joining us now is Detective Chief Inspector Peter Jones. Detective Chief Inspector, can you confirm that what was once reported by the police, to be a double suicide of a well-respected couple, is now a murder investigation?" asked the reporter.

"Our investigation is still ongoing," replied DCI Peter Jones, "but preliminary findings confirm that the deaths of Mr Trevor Johnson and Mrs Louise Johnson have been caused by a person or persons unknown to us at present. We are asking all persons who have been in contact with Mr and Mrs Johnson, in the last week, to get in touch with us at their local Police Station, or call this number shown at the bottom of the screen, as soon as possible. That's all the information I have, for now, thank you." He moved out of the camera shot.

Alan grabbed his mobile, dialled the 0800 number, and then resisted pushing the call button on hearing the reporter chance an offside question.

"Detective Chief Inspector Jones, do you have any further comment to make about the photos taken of Trevor Johnson with his various lovers?" the reporter asked, as she caught up with him.

The camera quickly panned around to include the DCI next to the reporter.

"I'm not aware of any such photos. Excuse me," he replied, then strode away.

Alan muted the TV, strode over to the sideboard, and opened the top drawer, took out the sepia-coloured scrapbook photo album, and then pushed the call button.

****

In her luxury apartment, in St George's Wharf, Rachel Stevens heard the name Trevor Johnson, whilst she towelled herself dry in the bathroom. She raced into the lounge to see the remainder of the news report, contemplating who to call first. Her professional reputation was at stake. It was just yesterday that her extraction team had delivered Trevor Johnson to her client, safe and well, although a little drowsy.

She made her first call.

"Domus House."

"Mr Joyce, please, tell him it's his daughter Rachel."

There was a short silence on the phone, and then, "Rachel. I trust you are well."

"Most content, Mr Joyce. I do hope that the parcel I delivered yesterday was undamaged."

"It was left in good condition, Rachel."

There was silence again. *Alexander Joyce had given his word that no harm would come to him, when she had dropped him off at his address in Chelsea,* thought Rachel.

"Thank you, Mr Joyce." The phone line went dead.

She dialled another number.

It was answered on the first ring. "Rachel, good of you to call."

"Can we meet, Andrew?"

"Funny you should ask. I was expecting the call. Vauxhall Bridge in five minutes."

The line went dead.

She donned her jogging gear and left her apartment.

At the security gate to her apartment block, she turned left and walked to the centre of Vauxhall Bridge and stood beside the familiar man. He was looking unkempt and tired, she thought, most unlike him. She turned her head to face him and smiled.

"Hello, Rachel."

"Andrew."

"I had a very pleasant lunch yesterday, Rachel, with a good friend of mine and told him that Trevor Johnson was safe and well."

"Indeed, he was Andrew. I have just had a word with my client who confirmed that he was."

"He was an asset, Rachel, his Intel was proving very useful to us, and now he and his wife are dead."

"I can assure you, Andrew, I played no part in his demise."

"I would like you to meet my good friend, Robert Fox. He is now a Private Investigator who has an interest in Trevor Johnson, or should I say, did."

"Where and when Andrew? I would prefer it sooner, rather than later; I do have a reputation to keep, and this kind of publicity does my credibility no favours whatsoever."

"He's in Brighton and I can hook you up with him tomorrow."

"Always fancied a trip to the seaside, Andrew."

"I shall arrange that you meet in front of the Pier at midday."

****

Charlotte sat bolt upright in the armchair beside the Hospital bed as the news report unfolded from the television. She hadn't slept well. Her mind was racing, thoughts dancing around her head as she tried to piece together the previous day's events.

Who was hidden in the bushes last night, who had sneaked into her home and what was she after?

She eased herself up from the armchair and slowly shuffled around the bottom of the bed towards the cabinet, where she picked out a little black book and returned to the armchair. Her body felt stiff and her head throbbed with pain caused by her head hitting the ground from the fall. She heard footsteps approaching her and looked up from reading her book to see the nurse stop at the bottom of the bed.

"Can't you sleep?" asked the nurse.

Charlotte grimaced in pain as she tried to straighten her back. "Just a bit painful," she replied.

"I'll get you something for the pain."

When the nurse turned away, Charlotte returned her attention to the little black book, thumbing through the pages until she reached a list of phone numbers.

She focused on one, committing it to memory, and closed the book. She tucked it into her dressing gown pocket, just as the nurse returned with a dispensing pot containing a couple of tablets.

She helped Charlotte into her bed, tipped the two tablets into her hand, handed her the beaker of water from the bedside cabinet, and watched her patient swallow the tablets.

Charlotte handed back the beaker to the nurse and laid down on the pillow and the nurse tucked her into her bed.

Charlotte was exhausted. She closed her eyes and began drifting off to sleep, reciting the phone number she had remembered. The nurse smiled and made a note of the drugs dispensed, closed the patient file and wrote the number that Charlotte was repeating over and over again in the top right corner of the cover.

****

Rosemary watched the newsfeed unfold. The news about the Johnson's death had already been relayed to her by Robert, but as far as she knew, there were only four people at the most who knew about the bedroom photos of Trevor Johnson; two of whom were dead, she was the third and the fourth can only have been the photographer. How did the reporter find out so quickly?

Her mobile rang.

"Hi, Rose. Have you been watching the news?"

"Yes, Robert, how did the reporter know about the photos?"

"I have been digging, Rose. I managed to look around the perimeter of the Johnson's home last night after I dropped you off. The place is being guarded at the front, at least, by the police, but I found one of the photos that you'd told me about hidden in the hedge at the rear of their place. It is singed around the edges, but I can clearly see Trevor frolicking on the bed with two women."

"If you could find the photo so easily, then so could the press," suggested Rosemary.

"I thought the same, but unless you scout or know the area well, you would never have seen the gap where I managed to get into last night, so this morning I contacted the news desk, before I phoned you, and asked a friend of mine who works on the editorial team, where the info came from."

"Go on, you've got me hooked, Robert."

"It had been delivered by hand to their office late last night, in an envelope left on the front desk, by a dispatch rider."

"Did they identify who it was, Robert?"

"No, the face was hidden, but my contact said it was definitely a woman."

"Could be that one of Trevor's lovers wanted her revenge. It doesn't help us though, we've lost our main lead, Robert."

"Yes, we have, however, I had a call from an old colleague who is the DCI running the investigation into the Johnson's death."

"The DCI on the news this morning?"

"The very same. I've informed him about our interest, and he told me that he had received a call this morning from another pupil from the school, Alan Manville, asking for help. He told him that he thought that his life was in danger and that he might be next, having seen the news about Trevor."

"By whom, Robert?"

"Don't know, Rose, but it's too much of a coincidence that when we are tasked to find the old headmaster, who just may have some insight into Derek Sargeant's death, the former pupils are suddenly in danger or dead. I also managed to sneak into the conservatory, where I scanned through the photo album that you mentioned. I've taken photos of each page, Rose. Every page is full of photos of Trevor and his family until Trevor's sixth birthday, then there are four pages where there are just photo corner mounts where photos were once secured, then on his eighth birthday, Trevor and his friends are seen in the photos again."

Chapter 10

The hot sun had burnt away the morning mist, which had been shrouding the Palace Pier in Brighton, to reveal a clear blue canvas with just a few wisps of cloud, high in the summer sky.

Rachel Stevens strode along the promenade towards the Pier, watching the various stilt walkers juggle balls and skittles between each other, whilst relishing the gazes from some of the walkers focusing on her skin-tight floral blouse and light grey, above the knee skirt; her choice of clothes accentuating her ample breasts, her slim waistline, and her long legs beneath.

It was a few minutes before midday, and as she reached the hot dog stand at the entrance to the Pier Gates, she spotted a familiar face from the week before, when her team had sped out the junction away from Trevor Johnson's office in Hays Mews. He was the man in the Ford Galaxy that they narrowly missed when their Range Rover turned out of Hays Mews. Their eyes had met, albeit for a moment, when she mouthed "sorry" to him, and she now felt an instant attraction towards him.

Her eyes targeted on his, and as they both stepped towards each other, she took in his rugged facial features, his short-cropped hairstyle, his clean-shaven square jaw on top of his athletic frame in a crisp white shirt, and light brown corduroy trousers. His brown brogue shoes were brightly polished; she did like her men well presented, and she wasn't disappointed with the opportunity to meet this man again. She hadn't, however, banked on the young pretty woman that she had just spotted out of the corner of her eye, signalling to him from the drinks stand opposite.

He turned briefly, and gave Rosemary the 'thumbs up', and then turned to face Rachel.

He spoke first.

"Rachel?" He committed her looks to memory, just as he had the first time.

"And you are Robert Fox," she replied, smiling at him. She held out her hand, which he shook with a firm, warm grip.

A tingle of excitement shot through her body as she kept her eyes locked on his. *Strong too*, she thought to herself. His eyes didn't waver from hers at that moment and for the first time in more years than she cared to remember, she was sexually aroused by a man. She wanted to be alone with him now, in a hotel room, together, intimately exploring his body. Her excitement quickly changed to disappointment when the cheery voice interrupted her thoughts.

"Hi," came Rosemary's voice from behind Robert.

"Rose. Let me introduce you to Rachel Stevens."

Rosemary held her out her hand, which Rachel shook, strong and hard with one swift downward movement, then released.

Her attention returned to Robert.

"I recognised you immediately from your photo and, if you remember, our brief encounter, the other day, Robert."

"Indeed. Your apology on the day is accepted, Rachel. Your reputation precedes you. I've heard that you are not to be messed with, and I do admire such a strong character in a woman."

Rachel's eyes locked on to his, stepping forward towards them both, she replied in a soft tone, just audible to Robert and Rosemary, "I presume that you are referring to Andrew's usual comment about me when he says that nobody fucks with Rachel Stevens." She smiled, seeing the disgusted reaction on Rosemary's face.

Robert nodded and smiled.

"But with you Robert," she continued, "I'd make an exception." There was a glint of mischief in her eye, which Rosemary clocked; her disapproval clearly noted.

"I'm off," Rosemary said curtly, "see you tonight, Robert."

"Let me know how you get on, Rose," Robert replied. He put his hand on her shoulder. "Look after yourself."

"I will," replied Rosemary, "nice to meet you, Rachel," Rosemary concluded, before turning on her heel, and briskly striding off along the seafront, towards Paston Place, which led to the Hospital. Robert watched her set off; she didn't look back. He turned his attention back to Rachel.

"Something I said?" asked Rachel, knowing full well that she had struck a chord with Rosemary's feelings. "My senses tell me that she's very fond of you, Robert."

"We are business partners, and we work very well together, as Andrew has no doubt informed you," Robert replied.

Rachel smiled, "I don't blame her, you know, for having feelings for you Robert, you're a bit of a catch."

"I'm flattered that you think so," he replied, dismissing the compliment. "Shall we get down to business?"

Rachel sensed that the man in front of her wasn't interested in playing games, sexual or otherwise, so she buried her thoughts of pleasure.

"Andrew has asked me to speak to you in private."

"So, tell me about your involvement with Trevor Johnson, whilst we enjoy the delights of Brighton Pier."

Rachel nodded, and he led her halfway along the wooden deck onto the west side of the Pier, where they sat together on the bench seating, against the railings.

"Let's start with the extraction team, and why Trevor Johnson was your target, shall we?" Robert asked.

"Okay," Rachel replied.

"My client found out that Trevor Johnson was bedding his mistress and her daughter, who I might add is over the age of consent. Photos had previously been taken of my client in the arms of his Chinese mistress, and he thought that it was Trevor who was attempting to blackmail him.

"My team were engaged to abduct him and take him to my client, who harmlessly, and I mean in a physical sense, coerced the information from him, and then satisfied that Trevor Johnson wasn't a threat, let him go. As I confirmed with Andrew, yesterday, he was alive when he was dropped off in a street by his home in Brighton.

"I have found out that the two Chinese women are employed by a Chinese virologist by the name of Tu Skreen Lee. They have been bed-hopping with several senior management figures within the pharmaceutical industries, accumulating information on their latest research projects through what is aptly named 'pillow talk', much of which has not been of any use to Mr Lee.

"My client, whose firm is far in advance of the others in relation to developing vaccines for highly contagious diseases, rumbled this and wanted some protection for his business and himself, approached one of his old Etonian friends who introduced him to one of his counter-intelligence friends from MI6. It transpires that Tu Skreen Lee was, in fact, a general in the Chinese army, before he took residence here in Britain. My client has been persuaded, shall-we say, to work with MI6, and he has since been feeding Mr Lee with credible disinformation about his work on the vaccines for some time."

"That's a dangerous game he's playing, Rachel."

"He's aware of that, but for all his faults and sins, he is loyal to the Crown. Robert, my client has been honoured with the MBE by the Queen for services to medicine. What's more, he is willing to sacrifice his own life for this country. The vaccine that his firm has developed may just be the answer to the ongoing Ebola crisis."

"How come there's no knowledge of this in the wider community, Rachel?"

"Quite simply, politics, power, and greed, Robert" – She paused, and then looked him directly in the eyes and requested – "Not a word that I have spoken, is to be repeated please, Robert?"

"It goes without saying, Rachel. What have we got ourselves into, Rachel?" asked Robert.

"Andrew and I have been asking the same question, Robert, and before you ask, I'm on your side. My team have been working closely with an agent named Rupert Brown from MI6, and have since yesterday, been the thread between the two Services, on this matter."

"What has Andrew told you about the enquiries we are making?"

"This is where it gets interesting, Robert. He tells me that you are searching for Trevor Johnson's old headmaster, Peter Dennett."

"We are. In truth, everybody believes he committed suicide in 1968, although there is no conclusive evidence either way. He too has secrets, which have come to light. He was one for the ladies, was Mr Dennett. He had numerous affairs, so it seems and even fathered a daughter, which he knew nothing about, who was born after his disappearance."

"Who has engaged you, Robert, his daughter?"

"No, we have been engaged by Jayne Sargeant who is the sister of one of the headmaster's pupils, Derek, who died around the time when the headmaster disappeared, and she believes that he is alive and knows the truth about her brother's sudden death."

"So who else knows about your investigation?"

"Why are you so interested, Rachel?" Robert was puzzled. Was Rachel keeping something from him?

"Just like to know if I can help you further, Robert."

"Well, so far, other than his daughter and Derek's sister, we have spoken to the only living teacher from the time, Charlotte Embling, as she was known by then, and Trevor's wife. We never did get to speak to Trevor, unfortunately, but his wife insinuated that Trevor had a dim view of his old headmaster, but she never let on why."

"Why was Trevor Johnson your person of interest, Robert?"

"Trevor was one of five boys, affectionately known as "The Heroes", at Plumpton Primary School, who each may have some tangible information about the sudden disappearance of Peter Dennett."

"So, where has Trevor's and his wife's death left you now in your investigation?"

"As of yesterday evening, we think we may have our next lead, another one of the boys at the school by the name of Alan Manville. He contacted Sussex Police after the news report of the Johnson's death. Apparently, he is worried about his own safety, for some reason, only known to himself, and wanted to speak to the police, urgently. He said that he knew Trevor well. He was advised to report to the nearest police station, but he never showed up.

"The police visited his digs in Timsbury this morning, but the place was empty. The police are still looking for him."

"Timsbury, you say?" Rachel asked. "He's not one of the heroes, is he though? So why does he think that he's in danger?"

"Firstly, no he isn't, but if this man, Alan Manville is Tu Skreen Lee's right-hand man, or was, he may be in real danger from the Chinese virologist, because of what he may know."

"Is he also an old pupil of Plumpton School, Robert?"

"He was, and there we both have a connection."

****

Standing at the nurses' station, Rosemary waited patiently for the charge nurse to arrive, having enquired about Charlotte's condition.

"Hello. Are you Rosemary Bennett?" asked the petite nurse.

"Yes, I am."

"I remember you from when you came in with Charlotte yesterday." The nurse paused. "You're the Detective from the Lanes, who helped my friend out last year."

"Did I? Who is your friend?" asked Rosemary.

"Jean Prentice and her husband, Trevor," replied the nurse.

"Jean is a lovely lady, she shouldn't have had to go through the torment that she did last year," replied Rosemary.

"You managed to deal with that despicable landlord of theirs. Getting back the money that he wrongly took from her was wonderful, and building the case for the police so the courts could put him away for what he put her through, was what saved her, so she tells me."

"I'm pleased that I could help her and her husband" – Rosemary responded, remembering the case – "Are Jean and Trevor okay, now?"

"I think so. She tells me that you believed her when nobody else did. She is always talking about you."

"Tell her I'm very grateful for her kind words," Rosemary replied, smiling at the nurse.

"You're after Charlotte Jackson?" the nurse asked.

Rosemary nodded, keeping Charlotte's maiden name to herself.

"I'm sorry to tell you that you have had a wasted journey. Miss Jackson discharged herself earlier this morning. You may have missed her calls. I saw her make several calls from her mobile before she left."

Rosemary double-checked her mobile, but there were no missed calls.

"Did she leave any message before she left?"

"No, not that I am aware."

"Okay, thanks for taking the time to see me." Rosemary turned to leave.

"Are you helping her too?" the nurse enquired.

"I hope so, she had a terrible fright yesterday," Rosemary let on.

"Oh?"

"I don't think she should be on her own at the moment," Rosemary pressed on, in the hope of gaining any further snippets of information.

"Well, I'm surprised she left this morning," the nurse continued, "because she was in a great deal of pain earlier. I remember giving her painkillers just before she dozed off for a while. She definitely had something on her mind; I heard her repeating a number, over and over again."

"I don't suppose that you remember the number, do you?" Rosemary asked.

"At my age, I'm lucky if I remember what I did yesterday," the nurse replied, laughing.

Rosemary laughed with her.

The nurse picked up the patient's file and pointed to the number in the top corner of the file. "That's why I always note anything unusual down."

Chapter 11

The fresh warm air, blowing gently off the sea, was a welcome relief for Rosemary, from the clinical smells of the hospital ward. Rosemary had tried the mobile number that she copied from the file onto her iPhone contacts list, but there was no answer.

She stood on the seafront overlooking Marine Parade, watching the Volks Railway carriages trundle along the single rail track which ran alongside Madeira Drive.

She had received the call from Robert to inform her that he had left Rachel Stevens on the Pier.

He bound up the steps and cosied up beside her.

"You okay, Rose?" he asked. She nodded.

"Didn't Rachel want to join us, Robert?"

Shaking his head, he replied, "Rachel has travelled worldwide, but has never visited Brighton. She's an interesting lady, Rose."

"You could say that. She certainly had her eyes on you, Robert."

Robert laughed. "She says I'm a catch, Rose, but I'm certainly not her type."

"Could have fooled me, Robert, after the comment she made about you being an exception to her rule."

"She wanted you out of the way, Rose."

"I could see that, as clear as a summer's day, Robert. She wanted you to herself," she teased.

"We needed to talk about the case on our own, as Andrew had requested. Besides, you are more her type."

"Oh?" Rosemary was taken aback. She considered herself a good judge of character but had clearly misjudged Rachel. "Perhaps we can arrange dinner with her if she is still in Brighton tonight?" Rosemary suggested.

"She's gone to meet someone in town, Rose. We'll catch up with her another day. So, any luck with the number, Rose?"

Rosemary shook her head. "I have dialled it three times; no one answered, so the line is still alive, but I didn't leave a message."

"I'll see if I can get any Intel on whose phone number it is," Robert replied. "Have you tried Charlotte?"

"A number of times, Robert, but there's no answer from her line, either."

****

Rachel Stevens felt the oriental masseuse's hands massage the oils into her tight shoulders, across her shoulder blades, and down her sun-kissed body to the small of her back, as she spoke on the phone to Andrew Braithwaite.

"It seems that all is not lost regarding the prospect of good quality Intel, from Tu Skreen Lee's research laboratory. His right-hand man, Alan Manville, is also one of the boys from the school back in 1968, and an old friend of Trevor Johnson, apparently. Alan managed to secure Trevor the account at Tu Skreen Lee's Research Institute.

"Alan phoned Sussex Police yesterday, after seeing the news bulletin about Trevor and Louise Johnson and asked to see someone urgently. He's since gone missing, and the police are trying to find him."

"I need you to find him, Rachel, alive preferably."

"Usual rates?" Rachel enquired as she turned to lay on her back, letting the masseuse's hands do their work.

"Is money all you think of?"

"Somebody has to fund my lavish lifestyle, Andrew," she replied.

"Okay, usual rates, but I want him alive Rachel."

The phone line went dead.

****

Charlotte had felt the vibration of her mobile through her handbag, which she was cradling against her stomach, as she sat in the front row of the upper circle seats at Watford Colosseum. The audience immediately around her stared at her in disgust for the continual disturbance of the solo performance. The piano recital of Frank Liszt's 'La Campanella' was in its final few bars when Charlotte's phone vibrated for the fifth time. She again tried to muffle the irritating buzz by smothering her bag with her cardigan, without success. Again, the audience close to her stared at her indignantly, making her feel like the runt.

She closed her eyes, wishing that the audience would just disappear and leave her alone. It wasn't her fault that her phone kept ringing, today of all days. She had received more incoming calls today than the rest of the year, put together. "Why me and why now?" she said to herself.

The phone stopped for an instant. This time, she looked straight ahead to her one-time Primary School student, playing the piano, and began to cry to herself, as the recital ended, the tears slowly flowed down her cheeks, and she grabbed a tissue from her bag and patted her face dry.

The pianist rose from the stool, and Charlotte stood with the audience to give rapturous applause.

The pianist responded with a deep curtsy. The pianist knew that her favourite teacher was watching her, from on high in the reserved seats for her invited guests and friends. She would see Charlotte soon enough, in her dressing room, backstage.

Charlotte was shown to the star's dressing room where a myriad of beautiful flowers were laid along the corridor outside of the dressing room door, the labels attached, congratulating Kimberley Honisett on receiving her lifetime achievement award at the international classical music ceremony.

The stagehand tapped three times firmly on the oak door. "Ms Honisett, your special guest is here."

The door swiftly opened. "Thank you, Paula." Her eyes fixed on Charlotte's and they both embraced each other. "Kimberley," Charlotte gasped, "you're squeezing me."

Kimberley released her bear-hug grip, allowing Charlotte to draw a breath. "Sorry Miss Embling, I forget my own strength, sometimes."

"It's all the time you spend in the gym, keeping yourself in good shape" – said Charlotte, smiling at the world-famous pianist – "Kimberley, your rendition was so beautiful. You were always going to be a star in the making when you were at school, and here you are an international icon. I am so proud of you, Kimberley Honisett."

"It's been so long since we last met Charlotte, in Poland, and I've never had the chance to thank you for what you did for me, in my time of need. You were my favourite teacher at Plumpton and I remember to this day what you told me then." Kimberley couldn't hide her adoration for Charlotte. "If it wasn't for you—"

Charlotte raised her hand to stop her mid-sentence.

"It was all worth it, Kimberley. I remember, to this day, saying to you, 'Be who you want to be', and look at you now, world-renowned, tall, slim and as I've always remembered from when you were eight, your lovely blond hair."

"Except the colour comes from a bottle now, Charlotte."

They both laughed. "Come in, come in," beckoned Kimberley, as she led Charlotte into her dressing room.

"It's just like in the movies," remarked Charlotte, as she took in the room full of brightly coloured bunches of flowers, bright light bulbs around the dressing-table mirror, the ice bucket holding the Moët and Chandon Champagne bottle, a scarf secured around its neck of a crisp white linen serviette, and champagne flutes already half-filled with the sparkling drink.

"I'm so glad you like it. The flowers that you see in here are not for me, Charlotte, they are from me to you, to say thank you."

Charlotte smiled warmly, took Kimberley's hands tenderly in hers and squeezed gently, as her gaze focused on her large hands and thick wrists, then on her bare muscular arms beneath the sleeveless evening dress.

"Thank you, Kimberley, but our meeting today comes with sad and disturbing news, I'm afraid. I've come to tell you that you, Alan, John and I may be in danger." Charlotte's eyes welled with tears. "Trevor has been murdered, as has his wife. I had a very lucky escape yesterday, and I fear that we are her next targets."

"Her?" responded Kimberley, "the killer is a woman?"

"I'm certain of it, but I'm not sure," replied Charlotte, "I also have to tell you that two private investigators are investigating the old headmaster's disappearance."

"Peter Dennett is dead to me, after what he did to me and my mother" — Kimberley said through gritted teeth — "and he can stay dead."

"I'm sorry, Kimberley."

"It's not your fault, Charlotte. You didn't know what went on then."

"What did go on?"

"It doesn't matter now."

"But it does, Kimberley, has this got anything to do with Derek?"

"No. Why?"

"It's just that Derek's stepsister appointed the two detectives to find out about Peter Dennett."

"Derek didn't have a sister, Charlotte."

"Apparently, he did."

"Don't tell me that Peter Dennett was the father?"

"I don't know."

"Why then, is she wanting to know so much about the old headmaster?"

"It's not her. Her mother wants to know if he is still alive. She's still convinced that Derek died because of the secrets he kept from her. She knew that there was something going on, but Derek said nothing."

"Karen Sargeant will always believe that it was someone else's fault."

"What if she is right, Kimberley?"

"Right about what? Derek's death or that the headmaster is still alive."

"Let's say both."

"You know what the coroner said. Derek died because of an unknown heart condition and the headmaster committed suicide, Charlotte. We discussed this years ago. Why bring it up now?"

"Because I was visited by the private investigator. She told me about Derek having a stepsister, and then I found out that you have a sister too, her father being Peter Dennett."

"You wouldn't have known that at the time, Charlotte; you left the school before she was born."

"You didn't tell me when we were in Poland, Kimberley."

"I'd rather forget, Charlotte, to be honest. Look, I shall always be grateful to you for helping me to turn my life around, but you can't change the past."

"I know. Sorry."

"No one knows that you are here with me, do they?"

"No one, I promise you. I called you from the Hospital on my mobile this morning. Nobody was around when we spoke."

"After all these years, and after all the operations, I thought that I had left the horror of Plumpton here in England, and Keith in Poland, for that matter. I didn't want to perform in England, and now I'm frightened that my sister may find out about me and that I may have to face that sperm of the devil, Abigail, again."

Chapter 12

Rosemary hadn't slept much overnight; she kept thinking about the attack on Charlotte at her home and what could have happened to her if she and Robert hadn't turned up.

'Who was the female assailant in motorcycle leathers and what did she want from Charlotte's home?' The question had been on her mind throughout the night.

Rosemary had managed to contact Charlotte, who had reassured her that she was safe staying in Watford with one of her friends, for a few days.

She eased her tired body out of bed, grabbed her phone to see that no messages had been left, and stumbled over her clothes that she'd dumped on the floor the previous evening. She shuffled into the kitchen to make herself a strong black coffee. Her sleepy eyes took in the messy worktops, which were cluttered with dirty plates and empty food cartons. She was happy on her own, enjoyed casual relationships rather than full-on.

Rosemary had tried to hook up with men of her age on dating sites, but she found that they were either on the rebound from previous relationships, cheating on their partners or wives, or just plain boring. At thirty-five, she thought of herself as reasonably attractive and well-kept, although not the same could be said about her flat. She couldn't bring any man back here, not that she ever wanted to, because they just weren't that interesting or exciting. She had embraced them all, just like the man she'd met last night, when they had first met at the usual local rendezvous, outside Café Rouge in the Marina, had dinner and spent time chatting about themselves.

Admittedly, Sam Rhodes was tall, rather handsome, and very chatty, but no sooner had she told him that she used to be in the police force, his tone had changed immediately. It wasn't until she got home after leaving him outside the restaurant that she found out he had been convicted of stalking the morning radio presenter, Judy Ramshaw, just over a year ago.

"Why can't I meet someone…," she said aloud to herself, as her mobile rang and the name illuminated on the screen, "like Robert."

"Hi Robert," she answered cheerily.

"Good morning. How was the date, Rose?"

"The less said, the better, Robert."

"Okay, Rose. What time are you meeting Jayne, Rose?"

"She's treating me to a late breakfast at the Half Moon pub, in Plumpton."

"Let her know we have a new lead; Trevor's school friend, Alan Manville, when we can find him, but don't be liberal with the information about him. I'm not too sure about that woman's true intentions, Rose."

"I'm wary of her myself, Robert, however, I'm more concerned about Abigail Wilton and her room full of memorabilia. It is rather unusual in my mind."

"Me too, Rose. Didn't Abigail tell you that she was, or still is, Chair of the Plumpton Historic Society?"

"Yes Robert, apparently so, since 1998."

"Have a dig around afterwards, Rose, see who else is or was part of the Society."

"Will do."

"I'm meeting with an old colleague who has information on the phone number that the nurse gave to you yesterday. Call me when you are finished, and we'll meet up."

"Speak later, Robert."

"Signing Off, Rose."

The line went dead.

****

Rosemary instantly recognised Jayne Sargeant sitting in the Saloon Bar of the pub, but this time in motorcycle leather trousers and a white tee shirt. Her hair was dishevelled. They shook hands and Jayne said, "I've ordered a full breakfast, Miss Bennett, hope that's okay with you."

Rosemary nodded.

"Dreadful to hear about Trevor Johnson and his wife," said Jayne, "I heard about them on the news. He was one of Derek's friends at Plumpton School when the headmaster was there."

"So I understand from our enquiries," replied Rosemary.

"Who would do such a thing?"

"I don't know. The police are investigating."

"Do you think he knew something about my brother's death or the headmaster's disappearance?"

"We shall never know. He was our primary line of enquiry, but that has been cut short."

"Don't tell me that he was your only line of enquiry, Miss Bennett? I am paying you good money to find out about what happened to my brother, and Peter Dennett is key to knowing why he died," Jayne responded, her voice raised above the level of the piped bar music in the background.

"No, he is not our only line of enquiry, Jayne, we are pursuing a number of leads around the country, to get the information that we need, for you, as quickly as we can."

"Well, it seems to be dragging on, Rosemary."

"It's only been a few days, Jayne."

"Nevertheless, I am expecting an answer and quickly. I would like to grant my mother her wish, preferably before she dies. It can't be difficult finding one old man. Do you have any idea if or why the headmaster disappeared?"

"We are gathering information from a number of sources, believe me when I say that Robert and I are both working hard on this, and as soon as we come up with something concrete, you will be the first to know."

"I hope that I shall be the only person to know, Rosemary," responded Jayne, curtly.

This meeting wasn't going to end well, Rosemary sensed.

"Of course," replied Rosemary. "You mentioned at our first meeting that your mother had a scrapbook photo album. Do you have it with you?"

"I do. What's so important about Derek's photo album?"

"I'd just like to see it, if I may, and take some photos of the pages if I may. It won't take long."

Jayne pulled out a thin sepia coloured scrapbook photo album and handed it to Rosemary.

"I'd just like to photograph each page if that's okay with you, Jayne."

Jayne nodded, then watched Rosemary as she focused the lens of her camera over each page, taking a snapshot in quick succession. Rosemary noted that there too were empty pages, save for the corner photo mounts, but took photos of them just the same.

The final photos taken were of the wooden cask on the easel supports in the church, Derek cocooned inside, then his headstone in the church graveyard. Rosemary glanced over to see Jayne's reaction, having seen the final images of Derek's life.

Closing the scrapbook, she thanked Jayne, handing it back to her.

They ate breakfast and Jayne chatted about herself mainly, before Rosemary footed the bill for the food and the two of them left. Rosemary walked with Jayne towards the only two cars in the car park, parked alongside a Yamaha motorbike. She noted the number plate of the motorbike, JAS 19.

"I need answers, Rosemary, and quickly," said Jayne.

"We do have a new line of enquiry."

Jayne stopped in her tracks. "I'm listening."

"One of the schoolboys has made contact. His name is Alan Manville. Did you ever met him?"

"No. My mother never mentioned him. I wasn't born in Plumpton. My mother sold the farm and moved to Stevenage soon after Derek's death."

"And your father?"

"He died before I was born."

"That must have been hard for you and your mum," replied Rosemary.

"She was devastated. Now I want to grant her dying wish; to find out why Derek died. The only person who can help me is the headmaster."

"You still believe he is alive?"

"My mother does, and he has something to hide, she's sure of it."

Chapter 13

The two-storey single dwelling opposite the Holy Trinity Church in Cuckfield was the home of Andrew Braithwaite, only known to a handful of people as his private home.

Robert Fox parked his Ford Galaxy in the driveway and killed the engine.

He saw the two cars owned by Andrew were backed into the garage, so he got out of the car, walked over to the garage and touched each of the bonnets, feeling the heat from the one on the right, indicating that Andrew had not long got home.

Turning his attention to the side window, into the hallway, he saw that the fresh vase of flowers which were usually displayed in the window, when he was at home, was missing.

He's with Linda, he thought to himself, and he turned back towards the driveway entrance and crossed the single access road, then walked through the iron pedestrian gate into the grounds of Holy Trinity Church.

He continued along the newly laid concrete pathway, which had been cast in a straight line between the gravestones, until he saw Andrew to his left, sitting on the wooden bench seat, in front of the single mature, hardy pine tree. Immediately to his right was his wife's headstone. He could see that Andrew had arranged flowers in the two glass memorial flower vases, to each side of the headstone and as was often the case, when he met him here, Robert could see Andrew's animated movements speaking to his wife. Andrew acknowledged Robert's presence, placed his hand on the headstone and bid "Bye for now my love." He stood up from the seat and walked the short distance to meet Robert.

"Fancy a coffee, Robert?" Andrew asked.

Robert nodded and they turned towards the exit that led towards the High Street, and into Andrew's favourite and the oldest coffee shop in the village.

"She was my one and only, was Linda," said Andrew, as they sipped on their hot drinks, "and I miss her, every day."

"I know how you feel," replied Robert sympathetically.

Andrew nodded, "Sorry Robert, of course, you do. I do believe Linda and Jenny are in a café up there somewhere, having coffee, just like we are now, looking down on us two."

They both fell silent for a few seconds.

"Robert, it's been eight years today since she died."

Robert nodded. "I didn't want you to be alone, Andrew, not today."

"You've always had my back, Robert, and thanks for coming. I do appreciate it."

They sat in silence again for a few minutes, each watching the world go by, out of the window.

"It's been more than ten years since you left the Service, Robert," Andrew said, "We made a great team, you and I."

"I was taught by the best, Andrew," replied Robert, "and you and Stewart believed in me when others didn't. I shall always be grateful to you, my old friend."

"You should have stayed, Robert…"

"I wasn't in a good place back then, Andrew," replied Robert, "not after Jenny's death."

Again, there was silence, and Robert recollected the day on which his beloved Jenny died.

He had been late meeting with his wife, having received the news that he was going to be a dad.

He cursed himself that, yet again, he had put his job first and his wife second. It wasn't that he didn't love her, he was just so immersed in his job, giving his all to his employer, the British Secret Service, its official title, or MI5, as it was more widely known, its mission, 'to protect this country from threats to national security such as espionage, sabotage, and subversion.'

'Regnum Defende' was written under the crest of the organisation's coat of arms, translated it meant defender of the realm, and he was proud of the fact that he did his role with passion, total commitment, and excitement. That was, until Jenny was mercilessly taken from him. She would normally meet him outside of the Royal Albert Hall, where he'd be waiting for her, with a single red rose in his right hand and a packed lunch on his left. They would cross Kensington Road, hand in hand, and sit together on one of the benches in Flower Walk, just behind the Albert Memorial – but on this day, he was late; 10 minutes late, to be exact.

He couldn't phone her to tell her he would be late, because the mobile phone signals had been blocked. He was running from Hyde Park Barracks on the north side of Kensington Road towards the Albert Memorial, where the traffic had come to a standstill, the ear-splitting cacophony of police and ambulance sirens filled the air, as they raced past him against the stationary traffic. He reached the pedestrian crossing to see Jenny waiting on the pavement outside of the old music hall, searching for him to her left and right. She turned her head to face front, seeing him wave to her and in that split second, she stepped from the pavement into the path of a speeding motorbike that had been weaving between the stationary traffic. She couldn't have seen it. The motorcyclist shouldn't have been speeding, he never had a chance of stopping, not at the speed he was going. He saw the motorbike run into her with such force that she was catapulted backwards towards the pavement, her head smacking hard on the edge of the kerb. The rider never stopped and never glanced back; he just raced away on the clear road ahead, into the distance out of sight.

Those few seconds that had turned his life upside down replayed in his mind in slow motion, every day at seventeen minutes after midday.

"Thinking of Jenny, Robert?" asked Andrew, as he placed a new cup of coffee in front of him.

"Sorry, Andrew. I zoned out for a second." He looked at his watch. 12.17 pm.

Andrew clocked him looking at his watch.

"That time will never escape us, Robert, when I was with Linda on our last day together. She took her last breath at 8 pm."

Again, a short silence.

Robert smiled at his friend, then changed the subject, "I rode up to Thunders Barrow from the stables the other day, with my new business partner, Rose Bennett."

"I heard that Stewart and Marcia have taken quite a liking to her."

"News travels fast," Robert replied, "she's a good one, Andrew; she just needs looking after. I sense that she has had a troubled past."

"Stewart says that Rosemary has taken a real liking to you, Robert."

Robert smiled, "Business partners, Andrew, nothing more."

Andrew acknowledged.

"I've enlisted Rachel Stevens to find the man who called yesterday. His name is Alan Manville, Robert. Alan was apparently a pupil at Plumpton Primary

School, so he says, although his name doesn't appear on any records as to him being there. However, Mr Manville has gone missing, as you know, and he is instrumental in us getting more information on Tu Skreen Lee and his laboratory. Lee is considered a real threat to national security, Robert. It appears that he and Lee have had a serious falling out, and he has suddenly disappeared, nowhere to be found."

"We would also like to talk to him too about the headmaster of Plumpton School," replied Robert, "he may be able to shed some light on what happened with Derek and the headmaster. At present, it's the only connection to the four remaining boys, known as the Heroes, which we have."

"Not quite Robert, that phone number you gave me, it's registered to a Kimberley Honisett, a famous pianist of classical music, by all accounts."

"I've heard about her," replied Robert.

"Well, here's the thing. Kimberley Honisett changed her name by deed poll in 2000. Her, or rather his, birth name was Keith Wilton."

"That's very interesting. So, what else hasn't Charlotte told us?"

Chapter 14

Rosemary weaved her car along the pot-holed farm track that led to Manville's Farmhouse.

Her thoughts were of Jayne's final words before she sat astride the motorbike. Having watched Jayne speed out of the car park, Rosemary enquired in the pub about the Plumpton Historic Society. Rosemary had found out that the former Chair of the Historic Society Committee, before Abigail took over, was Jean Manville, one of the oldest residents in the village.

As she stopped her car in front of the nineteenth-century stone building, the front door to the farmhouse opened, and out shuffled an elderly, frail woman. Rosemary stepped out to meet her and noticed the metal stirrup which was supporting her right leg.

"Mrs Manville?"

"Yes, and you must be Rosemary," the elderly woman replied.

Rosemary nodded.

"Thanks for seeing me at such short notice," replied Rosemary.

"Come in. How did you find me, Rosemary?"

Rosemary followed Jean Manville into the hall, then through to her kitchen.

"The innkeeper at the Half Moon told me where to find you. He said that you were the Chair of the Historic Society for this village."

"He took over running the pub from his father four years ago. His father and I were good friends, but I don't care too much for his son, I'm afraid. He's always thinking of himself, that one. Wouldn't trust him at all, let me warn you. Anyway, he's correct. I was until 1998. That was until Abigail Wilton arrived on the scene. The Society had lost many of its wealthy members, mainly due to them passing from this world to the next; I remember that we met at more funerals in 1997 than we did meetings. We lost six of our members in less than a year."

"I'm sorry to hear that," Rosemary responded.

"I was the only original member alive in 1998."

"Do you still attend the meetings, Jean?" asked Rosemary.

"No. Abigail Wilton is the only member now. Sadly, I resigned as a committee member in the spring of 1998, following an altercation with Abigail over the disappearance of some of the old School's photos and children's paintings. I remember them being posted around the hall walls one day and gone the next."

"Do you know where?"

"No, but I do remember the shadows cast on the walls where they were once hung."

Rosemary cast her mind back to the day that she was shown into the back room at Abigail's place, seeing paintings and photos hung on all the walls, wondering if they were the missing items.

"So, where and when did the Committee meet?" Rosemary asked inquisitively.

"We met four times a year at the village hall. Much of the memorabilia, including the children's writing desks were stored in the cupboard below the stage," Jean replied.

Rosemary had stopped at the quaint Hall, on her way from the pub. The walls were freshly decorated, and the shadows had gone. The hall was being set up for the weekend's cinema event and she had noticed that new chairs and tables were being wheeled out of the cupboard below the stairs.

She'd been greeted by the vicar and when she asked where she could find Jean Manville, several of the women standing nearby had fallen silent.

"There were twelve of us on the Committee of the Society, originally," Jean continued, "farmer's wives mainly, except of course Peter Dennett, the Headmaster of the school, who founded the Historic Society in 1960. Us girls, as he'd like to call us, would all bake cakes once a year and auction them to support the local charities. He used to judge all the cakes made, and the winner was rewarded with a rosette, which he would safety pin to our clothing at the summer fete, in front of the entire village folk, down on the Green next to the railway."

Rosemary seized upon the opportunity to ask more about Peter Dennett.

"Did you know Peter well, Jean?"

"Everyone knew Peter. He was tall, handsome, well-spoken and a saviour of the school. The children in the village have a lot to thank him for. Coming from farming backgrounds, the children, the boys especially, were only interested in harvesting, farm machinery, and livestock. Peter Dennett changed all of that; he made their learning fun. The children excelled at reading, writing, and arithmetic. Many have gone on to forge successful careers."

"He seemed to be the hero of the village, by all accounts, Jean."

"Yes, he was. All of the women swooned after him, even me, until he broke my trust in him."

"Oh, and how did he do that, Jean, if you don't mind me asking?"

There was silence just for a moment.

"It was something and nothing," replied Jean, "I don't really talk about it." Jean waved her hand dismissively.

"I'm sorry to pry," Rosemary replied.

"There's nothing to tell, really." Jean shrugged her shoulders.

Rosemary was hooked. She wanted to know what Peter Dennett had done to break this woman's trust.

"What was your favourite cake, Jean?"

Jean smiled broadly, and replied excitedly, "Lemon Drizzle. I won the cake making competition, in 1966, when I made my very first Lemon Drizzle cake."

"Do you still bake, Jean?"

"A little, but with these arthritic hands, I find that it takes double the time that it used to, not that my time now is spent doing much else. I made Lemon Drizzle yesterday. Would you like some?"

Rosemary feigned her excitement, "I would love some," she replied.

****

The motorcycle leather-clad woman was well placed in the field, across the track, opposite the farmhouse, to see through the kitchen window, at the two women seated at the large, old farmhouse pine table. She had chosen her spot well, hidden from view from the groups of ramblers, who were keeping to the footpath through the cornfield. She viewed through her binoculars the old lady placing the piece of cake in front of her guest.

She had been warned by the young innkeeper at the Half Moon pub, that a young woman was taking an interest in the Plumpton Historic Society, and that one of his regulars had told her where to find Jean Manville.

She kept her eyes firmly focused on the young woman, who she recognised as the same woman who had come to Charlotte's aid, the previous evening, when she had narrowly escaped from the policewoman at the old teacher's house.

She is becoming troublesome, she thought to herself, *this is the second time we have crossed paths*. She raised her portable listening device and concentrated on the conversation between the unsuspecting women.

****

"I can see why you won the competition," said Rosemary, in between mouthfuls of cake.

"Glad you like it; there's plenty more," replied Jean, elated that her guest was enjoying her cake. In her opinion, it wasn't a patch on how it had tasted in the past. "Perhaps another slice for you?"

"Yes please, I must admit I'm famished." Rosemary lied. She was still full up from the breakfast that she had eaten just a couple of hours before.

They talked for another hour about the village, Jean's farm, Jean's loneliness and her failing health, all the time, Rosemary munching on her cake, taking in the pictures of the farmhouse and milking parlour, hung on the wall, and the cookbooks on the shelves in the alcove beside the open fire.

"It was the year that England won the World Cup," Jean suddenly blurted out, shocking Rosemary with her outburst.

"Oh? What was that Jean?"

"When my cake won the competition," Jean responded.

She stared into Rosemary's eyes. A single tear ran down her cheek. Rosemary sensed that she was about to be told something which had been kept a secret for a long time. Rosemary saw the old woman's right-hand start to tremble.

"My husband, William, or Will as I knew him as, worked long hours daily, tending the farm, as well as his animals. I remember when the World Cup football was on that year, he postponed milking the cows or doing his daily chores for a couple of hours whilst he watched the games. He was a good man, caring, loyal and honest.

"We loved each other in our own way, but compassion and romance were not his things. By the time he had finished working on the farm, he would come home, sit at this table, and listen to the radio whilst I made him dinner, and then, more often than not, he would retire to that chair by the fire and fall asleep, until I woke him up and eventually, he would come to bed with me. Sometimes a woman has needs," she tittered, "and so when I wanted him to be amorous, all he did was fall asleep. A farmer's daily life is solitary, busy, long and exhausting.

I shall always remember the day when the new Headmaster greeted us at the school; his smouldering gaze hypnotised me, his compliments about my hair, my look, my body, sent a long-lost feeling of excitement through me. He did the same to all the women, I wasn't stupid, I knew that. When he announced at the first parents' evening that he was going to explore Plumpton's history and start-up a historic society, I, like all the other mothers, jumped at the chance of being on his committee.

"He was divine in terms of his rugged looks, his fashionable suits, his polished speech, and gentlemanly ways, quite the opposite of Will. I think he stole many women's hearts, did Peter Dennett."

"But not yours," Rosemary commented.

"No, not after what he did to me."

"Can you tell me about it, Jean?"

Jean hesitated.

Rosemary pressed on. "I'm just trying to get the measure of the man. You, yourself, said he was the saviour of the school, and that he was instrumental in bonding the village residents together. Him starting the Historic Society, organising, and heading the Village Fete, clearly, he was well respected, but not by you. Why was that Jean?"

"On the whole, he was a good man, but as I said, he did flirt with all the women."

"But he didn't with you."

"That's not what I said."

"What are you saying then, Jean?"

Again, Jean hesitated before she answered.

"I suppose it doesn't matter now that he's gone. It won't hurt him, but I still remember it as if it were yesterday. It was on the day that I won the cake making competition. The bandstand was emblazoned with England flags. The World Cup was ours and there was a flurry of euphoria throughout the village. All the cakes were placed on a table to the side of the bandstand, covered in netting to stop the birds and insects from landing on them. I was sitting with the rest of the farmers' wives in the front row of chairs, nearest to the bandstand whilst our husbands were busy harvesting the crops.

"The Green was full of children playing with each other, our little-un, Alan, was playing in his usual group on the roundabout, slide and swings, along with all the children, whilst the rest of the village residents had gathered to hear the results of the competition.

"I remember Peter Dennett bounding up onto the stage with a golden envelope in his hand, waving it to the enthusiastic crowd. He commented on all the cakes and then started the auction. Mrs Allcorn's cake accumulated most of the money at auction, and so I assumed that she would win the best cake award for the second year running, but she didn't; The headmaster called out my name. I couldn't believe it and couldn't wait to receive my rosette from the handsome Peter Dennett.

"I stood proudly on the stage as he paraded my cake across the stage in front of the crowd, everyone was clapping loudly, as he placed it on the silver cake stand on the table along with all of the trophies, and picked up the red rosette, proudly paced over and stood in front of me with his back to everyone else. He smiled at me and announced in a loud voice that everyone could hear, 'I present to you the coveted red rosette, Jean, for your truly wonderful cake.'"

The waft of his aftershave filled me with excitement. I hadn't been this close to him before and was taken in by his velvet voice and the sly wink of his right eye. It was as if no one else existed at that moment in time. It was just him and me.

He slipped his hand inside of my blouse, pulling it away from the skin, so as not to pierce my skin with the safety pin, so he told me. Then his fingers slid into my bra, the back of them brushing against my bosom, his thumb and forefinger gently squeezing my nipple, sending a wave of excitement through my body. William had not fondled my breasts for years and this yearning for someone to notice me had finally come in the form of the handsome school headmaster.

"I know it is unforgivable, but it wasn't the last encounter I had with Peter Dennett."

"Did you have an affair, Jean?" asked Rosemary.

"No, I did not," Jean replied. "Later that day. Will was busy in the fields, harvesting, but Peter knew that. He would have seen him high on the horizon, as he cycled to the farmhouse, I'm sure of it. I always blame myself for not chastising him when he touched my breast. I will never forget that day when he knocked on my door, invited himself in, closing the door behind him. He didn't say a word, he grabbed my waist, lifted me onto this table and we…"

Jean held her head in shame for a few moments, then raised her head, her eyes locking on to Rosemary's, then continued.

"Then he just left me on the table and walked out of the door as if nothing had happened. He'd ripped at my clothes; I remember feeling the sore skin from where they had been snatched from my body. After he left, I remember that I was almost completely naked. I didn't cry, I think I was too shocked to do anything except gather myself together, pick my torn underwear from the floor, and take myself off to the bathroom. I washed myself as thoroughly as I could, but to this day, I feel ashamed of what had happened. The next day, when I dropped my son, Alan, at the school, he approached me when I was alone, and apologised for what had happened, saying that it was all a misunderstanding and that I would understand."

"Did he rape you, Jean?" Rosemary asked.

"I don't know. It just happened."

"Did you tell William what had happened?"

"No, I couldn't take the risk of anyone knowing. Alan, even though he was not mine by birth, was my son and the last thing I wanted was to make things difficult between the headmaster and him at school, so I just let it go, never talked about it. Things happened like that in those days. Unlike nowadays, we just accepted it."

"You say that Alan isn't your son?" Rosemary asked.

"I couldn't have children. For that, I am grateful in a way. Can you imagine the reaction of the village if I had fallen pregnant and then told them who the father was? No, Alan's mum died in childbirth. I married Will when Alan was three years old and have endeavoured to be the perfect mother to him ever since. He says that he is proud to be a Manville, which means a lot to me."

"You say he is proud to be a Manville?" Rosemary queried. "But there's no record of his name on the school register."

"There won't be, Rosemary. I changed the name on the farm from Field to Manville's Farm two years after Will had gone, for tax reasons. Alan had his father's surname; the birth certificate and the school register records him as Alan Field, but he uses and signs off as Manville nowadays."

****

95

"Now, how did I miss that? The man I am looking for has changed his name. I'm looking forward to meeting you, Alan Manville. You are indeed a very resourceful woman, Rosemary Bennett. I shall be keeping my eye on you," said the woman, in motorcycle leathers, to herself, hiding in the bushes watching and listening to conversation unfold.

Chapter 15

Rosemary quickly scanned the kitchen again, whilst Jean Manville slid another segment of cake onto her plate and replenished both cups with fresh coffee. She spied the small, neat pile of Telegraph newspapers on the sideboard, to her left, together with a copy of 'The Scientist' magazine and a sepia-coloured scrapbook alongside them.

"Alan is a scientist, isn't he, Jean?"

"Yes, he is a virologist actually, and a very prominent one." She shuffled over to the sideboard and picked up the magazine and brought it to the table. "There is a feature about him in this month's magazine. He is so handsome, just like his father was at his age," she said, running her fingers over the photo of him on the front cover.

"You must be very proud of Alan, Jean. Does he keep in touch regularly?"

"It's funny that you should ask, Rosemary, because I was asked that just yesterday."

"Really? What a coincidence," Rosemary replied, eager to know more.

"Oh yes. A phone call from out of the blue from none other than Alan's old Primary School teacher, who asked me if I had heard from him lately?"

"Have you?" asked Rosemary.

"Why the sudden interest in my son, Rosemary?" Jean replied warily, "it seems a little more than a coincidence that first I am phoned by his old primary school teacher, who I've not heard from in over fifty years, and now you turn up on my doorstep." Jean was wary, Rosemary sensed it.

"I'm a Private Investigator and I'm looking into the disappearance of the very man that you have just told me about."

"Peter Dennett? Why him? When he vanished, there were several other people in this village, and the next, that wanted to know why. Some of the villagers were glad that he had gone, but you won't read that in any paper, or hear it from anyone who knew him, because all they cared about was the children's safety."

"What do you mean by the children's safety, Jean?"

"I've said enough, perhaps too much, and I'd like you to leave now, please."

"Okay Jean, but before I go. Have you heard of the Plumpton Boys?"

Rosemary saw Jean hesitate before answering. "No."

"Jean, he phoned the police asking to see them urgently, the day after Trevor Johnson and his wife were murdered. Why would he do that, Jean?"

"I don't know." Jean's reply was short towards Rosemary, "Now leave me in peace, please."

"I will see myself out, Jean, but you know my number if you want to talk to me again."

Rosemary stood and, on her way out, she dropped her clutch bag onto the sideboard, scooping it up quickly, together with the scrapbook she spied earlier and left the kitchen, closing the door behind her.

****

The motorcycle leather-clad woman, who remained still and silent, hidden away in the bushes, watched Rosemary Bennett leave the house, and drive away down the unmade road to the main highway.

"You may not want to tell Miss Bennett your secrets, but you will have no choice than to tell me," she whispered to herself, as she checked that ramblers weren't nearby, then left her cover, making her way back to her powerful motorcycle hidden from view behind the hedge in the next cornfield.

****

Rosemary was convinced that Jean Manville knew where her son, Alan, was holed up. She drove her car into the car park at the local convenience store at the top of the next hill. From there, she could see Manville's farmhouse. She dialled Robert's number; the call went to voicemail. "Robert, I may be on to something at Manville's Farm. Call me when you can." She ended the call. She quickly scanned through the scrapbook and found the blank pages where photos were once mounted, then pondered on whether to revisit the farmhouse. Seeing the natural stone and red clay-tiled building in the distance, then spotting the bunches of flowers outside of the shop doorway, she decided that she would, and offer Jean a bunch of the brightly coloured flowers, as a peace offering, as well as returning the scrapbook.

Her phone rang. She looked at the screen – it was Robert.

"Hi Robert, great to hear from you."

"Rose. I got your message. What have you found out?"

"Jean Manville remembers Peter Dennett, but for all the wrong reasons, Robert. I'll tell you more later when we have more time."

"Where are you, Rose?"

"I'm at the local store. I going to buy her some flowers and take them back to her, Robert. I think I left her on a bad note, so I'm going to say sorry, and return the scrapbook that I took."

"Does she know that you have it?"

"No, Robert, so I want to put it back before she misses it."

"Be careful, Rose."

"Will do."

"Signing off, Rose."

The line went dead.

The storekeeper welcomed Rosemary into her store and taking the flowers from her, wrapped them carefully in brown paper wrapping.

"Are you visiting someone in the village?" the shopkeeper asked, as she sellotaped the wrapping together and placed the wrapped flowers on the counter.

"Yes, I'm catching up with Jean Manville," Rosemary replied, "I suppose you know her and everyone else in the village."

"The older folk, especially," the shopkeeper replied. "Jean is known by everyone in the Village too. She is quite a character, is our Jean."

"Oh really? She seems to be very lonely in the farmhouse on her own," Rosemary responded.

"She was once very vocal when her Will was around," responded the shopkeeper, "but when he left her, for another woman in the village, she became withdrawn and unapproachable."

"I was led to believe that William or Will, as Jean calls him, died," stated Rosemary, now confused.

"Not Will, he's very much alive; he met up with another woman in the village before they both moved away."

"But Jean told me that she had to change the name of the Farm because of tax reasons, following his death."

The shopkeeper burst out laughing. "Is that what she told you, young lady? You be careful of that woman, she's trouble and make no mistake about it."

"So why did she change the name of the Farm?"

"Because she fleeced Will for everything he had, the Farm, his car repair business, everything."

"Why? I don't understand. She told me that she loves him and her son, Alan."

"Is that what she told you, too? Jean likes it when people feel sorry for her. Attention seeker, that's all that woman is. From the day Jean moved into the village, she has been nothing but trouble. Everyone around here knew her by her nickname when she was younger; 'Loose Elastic'."

"Oh?" Rosemary looked puzzled.

"In other words, she used to drop her knickers for any man, even the old headmaster."

"So, what about the story of the old headmaster and her?" Rosemary asked, wondering which storyline was true.

"Don't tell me that she told you about her and Peter Dennett?"

"She did actually, and in some detail too."

"He never had time for her, by all accounts. She threw herself at him, at every chance she got, but he rebuffed her every time. She could not accept that he wasn't interested in her."

"Jean told me that he was."

"I'm not surprised, you're new around these parts, aren't you?"

"Just like the others who visit her," came a voice from the back of the shop. "Are you her new carer?"

"No, I'm just visiting," Rosemary replied, turning to see an old lady supporting herself on two wooden walking sticks.

"Nobody just visits Jean Manville." said the old woman as she hobbled forward through the shopping aisle towards her. Her grey hair was combed straight, landing in a bob just above her shoulders, her make-up accentuating her high cheekbones and thin lips. She wore a summer flower three-quarter length dress and shiny white flat shoes.

"So, what business do you have with Jean, young lady?"

"I'm investigating the disappearance of the school's former headmaster, Peter Dennett," she responded.

"It's a bit late to be delving into what happened more than fifty years ago. You are clearly not the police, so who are you?" the old lady asked, stepping past Rosemary to stand behind the counter with the shopkeeper.

"My name is Rosemary Bennett and I'm a private investigator finding out why Peter Dennett disappeared."

"By none other than Abigail Wilton, I presume," said the old lady.

"No, my enquiries have nothing to do with Miss Wilton."

"Well let me tell you now that for all the lies that Jean Manville has told you, she had nothing to do with his disappearance, because on the night of his disappearance, she stayed here with me and my children, spinning the same old yarn that she has probably told you, and I, like you, fell for her lies and took pity on her, which is why you are buying flowers; am I right?"

Rosemary nodded.

"Well, there's no pity paid to her anymore. She has spread her lies far and wide, and that's why people around here keep their distance, and I suggest you do the same."

"How do you know her so well?"

"I'm Deborah Branning and this is my daughter, Chloe."

"I'm trying to see the connection?" questioned Rosemary, now more confused than before.

"If you'd care to join me in the back garden for a cream tea, Rosemary, I have a great deal to tell you."

Rosemary smiled. "I'd like that," she replied.

"Chloe, put those flowers back in the pot. I don't think our guest will be needing those after I tell her everything about our Jean."

"Okay, Mum. I will be shutting the shop in ten minutes, and then I shall be popping out Mum, but I won't be back late."

"Okay love, but you take care on the roads."

"I will."

Rosemary looked puzzled at the fact that the only shop in Plumpton was closing at 1.30.pm.

"In Plumpton, we still shut half-day on Wednesdays," Mrs Branning clarified.

Holding out her arm to Rosemary, she asked, "Would you be a dear and help me through to the garden? As you can see, my legs are not what they used to be."

Again, Rosemary smiled, nodded, and tucked her arm under Deborah's armpit and helped her through the shop. "In answer to your question, Rosemary, the connection is that my son, John, is Alan's best friend."

They sat in the garden chairs at the large mosaic tiled table. Chloe brought them out a cream tea.

"See you at teatime, Mum."

Deborah waved to Chloe and watched her leave by the back gate.

There was a sudden roar of an engine, the noise deafening at first, then dissipating as it raced away into the distance.

"Chloe's forty-six and she still rides that motorbike like she is a teenager. Shall I pour?" asked Deborah.

"Please do. This is very kind of you to spare me your time," Rosemary responded, her mind focused on the noise of the motorbike. She'd heard a similar roar at Charlotte's.

"Can you tell me about the boys, Mrs Branning?"

"Nothing to tell, really. They were just boys having fun, growing up together, and playing together."

Rosemary took the school photo from her bag and placed it on the table in front of her host.

"Do you remember this photo?"

Deborah Branning studied the photo carefully before answering.

"Yes. Where did you get it?"

"I printed it from the Historical Archive."

"I used to have one just like it in the family album, but I gave it to John when he left to join the Navy. He's currently serving his final year as Captain on board HMS Victory in Portsmouth."

"Do you and Chloe keep in touch with him regularly?" Rosemary asked.

"We both do. Why do you ask?"

"As I said, I'm investigating the disappearance of the headmaster, Peter Dennett."

"He's long gone. Hasn't been seen since 1968. Have you tried contacting the teacher, Charlotte Embling? She moved to South Africa at the start of the summer in sixty-eight, so you might have a job tracking her down if she's still alive."

"Thanks, I will. What of the other boys, Keith and Alan?"

"They've all gone their separate ways, and they don't contact each other now. You must know how it is."

"Yes, I do. I can't remember when I last contacted one of my old school friends."

****

Jean Manville heard the roar of an engine coming from the front of the house. The front door creaked open, then the sound of footsteps pacing towards the kitchen through the hall.

"Did you forget something, or have you come to apologise?" she asked in a loud voice.

"No, not me," came the reply.

"It's you. What do you want?" asked Jean hesitantly, "You are not welcome here."

"Thought we'd have a little chat."

"What about?"

"You know, Jean."

The kitchen door slammed shut.

"Please. I've done nothing wrong," came the cry from Jean, and then silence.

Chapter 16

The very familiar face raised her finger, pressing it to her lips. "Be silent, Jean," she told her menacingly. "Where's Alan?"

"I don't know. I haven't spoken to him."

"Really? But you just told Miss Bennett that he spoke to you yesterday."

"You were listening?"

"Every word. You need to be careful what you say. Walls have ears, Jean, and that yarn about Will being dead—"

"He is dead to me. He left me for that woman, and they both took my son away from me too!"

"He's not your son though, is he, Jean? He's William's."

"He is mine. I treat him and love him as my own."

"Until his dad saw you and the headmaster on the table, Jean."

"He did not." Jean's mind started to spin as she remembered that day. *Will couldn't have. He was ploughing the fields*, she thought to herself.

"He collected his son from school because you told him to fetch him and take him over the fields, but he came back with him early, to find you shagging the headmaster on the kitchen table."

"But—"

The visitor bared down on Jean Manville, who was sitting in Will's armchair in front of the open unlit fire, their noses almost touching. Jean could smell stale alcohol on the unwanted visitor's breath.

"I know more about you than you think. You've ruined many good relationships in this village, you twisted old woman," the visitor spat at Jean. "Now I want to know what rumours you have been spreading about me."

"I don't know anything, so just leave me alone," Jean replied, her eyes full of fear.

"I heard you on the phone to someone earlier, telling them that I murdered Trevor and his wife."

"I didn't."

"You did Jean, I heard you, just like I heard you talking with the private investigator just now. Who were you talking to, Jean?"

"No one."

"Okay. Let's try this question. Where's the envelope?"

"I don't know what you're on about. What envelope?"

"Don't try my patience, Jean."

"I don't have the envelope," Jean replied, suddenly realising what she'd said.

"So, you do know. Where is it, Jean?"

"I don't have it, I never have."

"You know what's inside it, Jean?"

"I don't, believe me, I don't."

"I asked Trevor where it was too," the visitor said to her with a devilish grin, "and you and everyone else knows what happened to him and his wife. She was so in love, poor thing, or so she thought until I delivered her an envelope of my own."

Jean's eyes widened with horror, hearing what her unwanted visitor said.

"It was you! you murdered them! For what, an envelope?"

The visitor nodded.

"Not any envelope, Jean. My envelope."

"I've told you; I don't know where it is."

"Where's Alan's scrapbook, Jean?"

Jean looked over to the sideboard. The visitor's eyes followed hers.

"It's not here," replied Jean, surprised to see it gone, "and you'll waste your time looking too." She gave a wry smile when she realised that the only person who'd been here since she left it on the sideboard was the private investigator.

"Then, perhaps Alan will tell me where I can find it."

"You leave Alan alone. He knows nothing."

"You were talking with him on the phone the other day, I heard you."

"It wasn't him."

"So, who was it then, Jean?"

"I won't tell you."

Jean kicked out her legs, her metal stirrup around her right leg struck her visitor's shin. Her visitor screamed out in pain, recoiling backwards out of harm's way, towards the open fireplace.

The visitor's back smacked against the mantelpiece and she roared in anger, as her arms fell to her side, her right hand touching cold metal. A wry smile appeared on the visitor's face.

Jean's eyes suddenly filled with fear as she saw her visitor grab the poker that was hanging from a hook by the open grate, then hearing the woman's battle cry, she knew what was coming. She was too frail to move out of harm's way, as the woman leapt towards her, raising the poker above her head, bringing it down hard on Jean's head splitting Jean's skull. Jean immediately saw the blood mist in her eyes, then darkness. The poker repeatedly smashed down on Jean's skull until the violent anger of her visitor dissipated. Then silence.

The visitor stood motionless for several minutes, staring at Jean's caved-in head, cranked backwards over the backrest of the chair, her mouth agape. A pool of blood was now coagulating on the floor behind and below the chair.

The visitor felt no remorse, no disgust, just sheer determination to find the package.

She searched all around the farmhouse for the envelope, to no avail.

She opened all the doors to the rooms in the farmhouse and returned to the kitchen, where she grabbed the crochet blanket from the sideboard and the half-full whiskey bottle and stepped over to Jean's chair. She draped the blanket over her head and body and doused it with the alcohol.

Returning to the table, the visitor scrunched up the newspapers laid out across it, stepped across to the gas cooker, lit all the rings and using one sheet of paper lit it and held it aloft like an Olympic flame. She carried it over to the draped body and set light to the blanket. She quickly grabbed the New Scientist magazine, paced over to the door, opened it and, not looking back, closed it behind her as she left.

Placing the helmet over her head, she started the motorcycle and roared away.

****

Deborah Branning refilled Rosemary's cup with hot tea from the teapot. "Why now, after all this time? Peter Dennett has been dead for more than fifty years; no one has taken an interest before now."

"There has been some new interest in the sudden death of Derek Sargeant, and it is believed by parties, who shall remain nameless, that Peter Dennett is still alive, and that he may have further information on how he died," Rosemary replied.

"Everyone knows how Derek died. The coroner at the time confirmed it," said Deborah, "and as for the headmaster, he jumped off the cliffs at Beachy Head. Somebody is wasting your time and their money. I can't help you any further, I'm afraid."

Deborah rose from her chair, which Rosemary took as a sign that she had outstayed her welcome.

"Maybe, Mrs Branning, but I've been asked to investigate all the same. There is one other thing that you may be able to help me with," she said as she reached the rear gate leading to the rear car park.

"If I can, I shall try," replied Deborah.

"Before Derek died, he told his teacher that he'd seen spacemen. Do you know what he meant?"

Rosemary watched Deborah carefully, awaiting her response. She saw Deborah's eyes dart down and to the right.

"No idea. The boys used to tell me about the spacemen in the barn at Sargeant's Farm when they came round to play, but I never saw anything untoward. If my memory serves me right, there was a ferocious fire inside of a barn on their farm," Deborah recollected, "because the fire engines raced past the shop, and from the upstairs bedroom window, I could see them speeding towards the farm."

"Who owned the farm, Deborah?"

"Karen Sargeant. That poor love. Derek died a couple of weeks later."

"Do you think that the goings-on at the barn had something to do with his death?" asked Rosemary.

"No, as I said, it was confirmed as an undetected defect in his heart. I wouldn't be surprised if his father had the same defect."

"Who was his father?"

"Roger."

"They had just one child, did they?" Rosemary asked.

"Yes, just Derek. Then about a month before Derek died, Karen's husband, Roger, left her. A few months after that, she remarried."

"Karen did?"

"Yes, they had a daughter, I'm told. Her name's Jayne."

"Who did she marry?"

"None other than William Field."

Chapter 17

It was still light in the late evening when Rosemary bid farewell to Deborah Branning, and following the revelations, decided not to return to Manville's Farm immediately, but return the scrapbook to her in the morning.

Rosemary checked her phone but there were no missed calls. She clicked on Robert Fox's number, and let it ring until it went to voicemail. "Hi Robert, just checking in. Call me when you can. We should catch up at the office, I'm definitely on to something." She ceased the call and promised herself that she would ring him later.

Back at her flat, she undressed down to her underwear and busied herself tidying away her clean clothes, which she had piled up on the ironing board in the box room, changed the bed linen which hadn't been done in ages, separated her whites and coloured clothes and placed the coloured into the washing machine. Clearing the kitchen was an effort for her, as she hated the smell of old food scraps.

Finally, she spent some time cleaning the bathroom, which hadn't seen a cleaning cloth for days and whilst rinsing down the bath after cleaning off the tidemarks around it, thought of the day's events.

The elderly women undoubtedly had eventful lives living in the village. The women she had met today, each had a child, who they worshipped, and all had their lives touched by good and bad men.

She turned off the shower and standing up to stretch her back, turned and looked at herself in the mirror. She shook her head and chastised herself for not looking her best.

She ran herself a hot bath, adding a calming liquid into it, stripped off, and sunk her body into the steaming hot water. She laid back, letting the hot water lap over her body and shut her eyes, letting her thoughts of the day fade away.

****

A constant banging on the shop front door awoke Chloe Branning.

In her nightgown, she quickly paced through the shop, cricket bat in hand and unlocking the door, flung it open to be greeted by two policemen.

"You won't be needing that with us, madam, and anyway, it's not a good idea to greet anyone with the intent of committing a criminal act," said the policeman, facing her.

"It's half-past eleven, so don't you think that I would want to protect myself at this ungodly hour from people beating our front door down? What do you want, Officer?"

The senior of the two officers smiled and said, "We are sorry for the intrusion at this hour, but we are asking everyone in the area whether they heard anything unusual at Manville's Farm earlier today."

"Can I ask why, Officer?"

"There's been a fire—"

"Who is it, dear?" came the voice from the back of the shop.

"It's the police, Mum. There's been a fire at Jean's farm, and they want to know if we heard anything unusual earlier today."

"Is Jean okay?" the old woman asked.

"Is there a reason why she shouldn't be?" replied the policeman.

"We know that she is very frail. Chloe delivers the newspaper to her every morning," replied Deborah Branning.

"And she was okay this morning, was she?" asked the policeman.

Chloe first looked at the policeman and then at her mum.

"She was fine and in good spirits this morning, when I left her."

"What time was that?"

"Eight-thirty," replied Chloe.

"I suppose you wouldn't know if she had any visitors today?"

Deborah Branning was quick to respond. "She was visited by a young woman."

"Yes, that's right Mum. She came to see us too, didn't she Mum?"

"That's right dear. Go and put the kettle on Chloe."

"Okay Mum," Chloe replied.

"Do you happen to know her name, Mrs Branning?"

"Rosemary Bennett, I think she called herself."

"She bought some flowers, Mum," came the shout from the kitchen behind.

110

"That's right Chloe, now concentrate on making the tea and don't burn yourself on the kettle."

Deborah stood in the doorway. "I would let you in, but Chloe doesn't like visitors after dark. She thinks that they are here to hurt her. Her mind isn't quite right, poor love."

"I understand Mrs Branning. Miss Bennett bought some flowers, did she?" asked the officer.

"She did, similar to those there in the pot," replied the old woman, pointing to the bunch of mixed flowers, "she told us they were for Jean. She'd been visiting her already earlier today and was going back to take her some flowers."

"What time would this have been?"

"About one o'clock."

Both officers looked at each other.

"Are you sure of the time, Mrs Branning?"

"Quite sure," she replied, "the shop closes halfway through the day every Wednesday, at half-past one, and she bought them just before we shut the shop."

"Do you know if Rosemary Bennett was a relative?"

"I don't think so. The only people we know directly related to Jean are her ex-husband, William and her son, Alan."

"We haven't seen her before, have we Mum?" came Chloe's voice from behind. "Here's your tea Mum."

Deborah looked over her shoulder at Chloe, took the mug from her daughter and smiled.

"Thank you, my sweet. Now get back to bed. You have got to be up bright and early tomorrow morning. I shall lock up, the policemen are just leaving."

Chloe kissed her mum on the cheek, turned and walked through to the back of the shop and out of sight.

"One more question before we leave, Mrs Branning. Were the flowers paid for by card payment?"

"No, she paid cash. Now if that's all, I am very tired, and we have a shop to open in seven hours' time."

"Of course, Mrs Branning. Thank you for your assistance at this late hour." The policemen turned to leave.

"In answer to your first question, Mrs Branning, Jean Manville, unfortunately, perished in the fire."

Deborah Branning feigned an expression of horror on her face, and then closed and bolted the door.

She hobbled back into Chloe's room, her walking sticks clipping the vinyl-tiled surface.

"Have you been misbehaving again, Chloe? How many times have I told you not to go to Manville's Farm!"

"I haven't, mum."

"Don't lie to me child, you are always causing trouble up there," Deborah scolded, as she raised her hand, thrashing her walking stick in her right hand down on Chloe's back.

Chloe knew what was coming and she stuffed the corner of her pillow into her mouth, suppressing her cries of pain with each beating, as she knew that she would suffer more blows if her mother heard her cry.

Chapter 18

The noise inside of Rosemary's head was ringing. Sleepily, she raised her head just enough to see the mobile screen illuminate, the number on her screen unfamiliar. Her old bedside clock's luminescent hands pointed to just after midnight, and she had been asleep for less than two hours. She made a grab for the phone and thumbing the accept button, raised it to her ear.

"Hello?"

"Miss Bennett, DCI Peter Jones here."

The name didn't register. "Sorry, who?"

"Miss Bennett, I am investigating the sudden deaths at Trevor Johnson's residence..."

"Yes, of course," replied Rosemary, wondering why he would be phoning her at this hour, "um, it's midnight Detective Chief Inspector?"

"Yes, I know," he replied, "Miss Bennett, I would like you to come down to the station please, there's a car waiting outside for you."

"Now?"

"Yes please, Miss Bennett. I would like to talk to you immediately about your visit to Manville's Farm. There's been an incident and I would appreciate you coming to the Police Station, so we can discuss your visit there today. The officers outside will bring you here."

Rosemary racked her brain as to why and how, he knew she'd been to see Jean Manville.

"I need to get myself dressed. I shall be there in a few minutes, DCI Jones."

"I understand Miss Bennett, just to remind you that there is a car waiting for you, my officers shall look after you, so please be as quick as you can."

The phone rang off.

She peeled the bed covers off herself, swung her legs out, and slowly shuffled over to the window. Sure enough, a Police car was parked on the opposite side of the road with its internal light switched on.

Rosemary's head was buzzing with questions and reliving the events of the day. She donned her tracksuit top and bottom, tussled her hair to remove its bed head shape, splashed water over her face, and then grabbed her bag on the way to her front door.

At the bottom of the stairs, she pulled open the front entrance door and the cold midnight air stung her face. A Policeman was waiting by the entrance door on the pavement in the otherwise empty street.

"This way please, Miss Bennett," called out the policeman.

The streetlights suddenly flickered, momentarily plunging the street into darkness, making Rosemary stop.

"This way please," the policeman said, motioning her to the open rear car door.

There was a crackle on the policeman's radio. Then she heard the message.

"Caution, the detainee may be carrying a weapon."

Rosemary instantly saw the policeman's reaction and drawing his baton, commanded, "Face the car and place your hands on the roof now!"

"There's no need for this," responded Rosemary, as she obeyed the command, "I'm not carrying a weapon."

"Stand still and don't move," shouted the officer. Grabbing the rigid speed cuffs, he snapped one cuff around Rosemary's right wrist, pulling it down harshly to the small of her back, then grabbed her left, placing them both in the restraints.

"There's no need for this, your DCI said that you would look after me," Rosemary repeated, smarting at the pain from her wrists.

"You're under arrest!" The standard arrest procedure continued, the policeman's voice just a blur to Rosemary, as she saw the lights from the flats above, and opposite flick on, and the curtains and blinds behind the neighbours' windows twitching. It wasn't the first time that over-zealous police officers had arrested her and dragged her into a car from outside of her flat. The policeman guided her into the back seat. Then sat beside her, gave his cue to the driver and the car sped away, its blue lights strobing across the building facade.

****

Robert had been awake for less than ten minutes, slowly coming to, following the previous day's drinking binge with Andrew Braithwaite.

Sipping his hot tea, standing at the bay window of his seaside mobile home, he watched the police car slowly meander its way down the winding tarmac road, stopping outside his plot.

Constable Berry stepped outside of the car and proceeded to his front door.

Opening his front door, he greeted his unannounced visitor.

"Morning, Trish."

"Morning, Mr Fox. Looks like you have had a heavy night on the booze."

"Call me Robert, Trish, and yes, it was. I was remembering old times with an old colleague. What brings you here, Trish?"

"It's your partner, Rosemary Bennett. She's been detained at John Street, something surrounding the fire at Manville's Farm, in Plumpton; she also resisted arrest apparently, according to the charge sheet."

The news focused Robert's attention immediately.

"You better come in, Trish."

"No time, Robert. I should not even be here, but when I saw Miss Bennett brought into the station earlier by the two officers, she wasn't her best. At the desk, they said something about her being seen immediately before the fire started at the Farm."

"What time did the fire start, Trish?"

"Not sure, the fire investigating officer's opinion is that it started between the hours of one and three yesterday afternoon."

Rose had phoned Robert at around one o'clock saying that she was at the local shop, Robert recollected to himself.

"How come you're out this way, Trish? John Street's off your patch."

"I know. We were called in to help with crowd control at the gig on the seafront last night, and we had been summoned for an early morning debriefing, with the new Chief Superintendent. On my way out of the station, I saw them bring in Miss Bennett. Her arrest was all wrong, Robert. You know I am a stickler for the rules, well this just didn't seem right. I did see the DCI, who had arranged the soft pickup, but orders from on high had elevated the pickup to hard detention."

"Do you know who gave the order, Trish?"

"No, and I didn't ask."

Robert could see the concern on Trish's face. "I shall get myself over there and find out what's been going on."

"You're in no fit state to drive Robert, do you want a lift?"

Robert smiled. "I thought you were a stickler for the rules, Trish?"

"Let me just say I owe you a favour for not bad-mouthing me, when I arrested you the other night."

"I'll get my coat, Trish, and thanks."

The flashing blue lights of the police car made it a speedy journey to John Street Police Station, on the east side of Brighton, through the heavy commuter traffic, which brought Peacehaven and Rottingdean to a standstill each weekday morning.

Robert scolded himself for not taking the missed calls or answering Rosemary's messages. He'd not looked at his mobile once whilst he was with Andrew, only listening to his messages when he got home, leaving it until the morning to phone.

He punched in the number for Andrew Braithwaite, during the journey, asking him to help in Rosemary's release.

"I shall drop you at the junction of Edward Street and John Street, Robert. It wouldn't do me any favours if they knew I'd brought you here."

"Thanks, Trish," Robert replied gratefully, shaking her hand, "I owe you one."

"Pleasure is all mine Robert; I know a good guy when I see one. Rosemary is lucky to have you on her side."

Robert smiled back at her, stepped out of the car, closed the door gently, and walked the short distance into the Police Station. He couldn't believe that he hadn't been there for Rosemary, just like he wasn't there on time for Jenny, when he should have been.

Chapter 19

Robert's phone rang, to the annoyance of the young desk officer, who pointed at the poster on the wall opposite, which read, 'Do not use mobile phones in here'.

He headed out of the station, taking the call.

"Robert Fox." he answered curtly.

"Robert, it's Peter Jones."

"Why has Rose been arrested, Peter? There had better be—"

Peter Jones interjected, "Robert, I can't explain now. Meet me at the end of John Street, by the Courthouse."

The phone rang off.

Robert checked his watch as he approached the Courthouse; it was just after nine-thirty and the usual traffic congestion along Edward Street was subsiding, however, the smell of exhaust fumes still lingered in the damp morning air.

The siren of an ambulance racing towards him from the bottom of Edward Street drew his attention and he watched it race past him, up the hill. He closed his eyes, and his thoughts tumbled back to that fateful day when Jenny was taken from him so mercilessly; the day he let her down, just as he had done with Rosemary.

"Robert."

He smiled, recognising Rosemary's voice, opened his eyes to see her and the DCI, pacing towards him.

"Hi Robert, I am so glad to see you."

"You okay, Rose?"

She nodded. "What did you say to the police, Robert?" she asked.

The DCI laughed, "Whatever you said, Robert, has rattled the Chief Superintendent."

"I called in a favour from my colleague in five and asked him if he could help."

"Some favour, the Chief Superintendent is bloody fuming," the DCI replied, "it's all round the station."

"Go on," replied Robert.

"Firstly, Robert, I'm probably partly to blame. I phoned Rosemary and asked her to meet me at the station. I sent a car for her and let the desk officer know that she was helping me with the investigation into the Manville Farm murder."

"Murder?" Rosemary questioned.

"Indeed," replied the DCI. "Jean Manville was bludgeoned to death before the kitchen in the farmhouse was set alight. You had been seen leaving Manville's Farm shortly before the fire started, and that is why I called you and arranged for a car to collect you and bring you to the Station, so we could talk about your visit, before things spiralled out of control."

"I told Walker and his sidekick that I had been there but had left shortly after one o'clock," stated Rosemary. "I remember the time because I was at the local store about ten minutes before they closed at one-thirty, as they do at the Village Store, every Wednesday. I could see the Farmhouse from the Store's car park on the hill, but there was no sign of fire then."

"Walker maintains that you purchased some flowers for her, and then returned to the Farmhouse," said DCI Jones.

"I did not," exclaimed Rosemary.

"The shopkeeper's mother, Deborah Branning, said that you did. Walker got to hear of it first-hand, as he was at John Street at the time. I told him I had sent a car to collect you, and he told me to stand down as he was taking over the investigation. Apparently, he knows Deborah Branning well. He informed the arresting officers that you were trouble, and to expect hard resistance."

"He bloody would, wouldn't he? He has an axe to grind," Rose vented.

"You know him, Rose?" asked Robert.

"You could say," replied Rosemary, "he's the reason I left the force."

"Why?"

"In those days, Chief Superintendent Raymond Walker was no more than a Detective Constable himself. I transferred from Haywards Heath to Brighton as a Detective Constable. At first, it was great, working with him on the various cases. We even solved the jewellery heist that happened in Seaford at Trubshore's Jewellers."

"That was ten years ago, and as I remember, it was the policewoman who got the credit. Was that you?" asked the DCI.

Rosemary nodded.

"But, her name was Chandler, Rosemary Chandler," The DCI replied, looking puzzled.

"That was me. I changed my surname back to my maiden name as soon as I left the force."

"You've been married, Rose?" asked Robert. Now they both looked puzzled.

"My late husband, Tim, was shot during the 'Holly Croft' siege the day after we returned from our honeymoon."

"I didn't know Rose," replied Robert.

"Neither did I," responded the DCI.

"It's not common knowledge," Rosemary stated, trying not to make eye contact, "but that's not the half of it. The work was piling up and I ended up staying late, ploughing through the files, most of the time on my own, and on occasions with Walker.

"Then, one night, there were just us two in the office. He started talking about his long-suffering wife and how she didn't understand why he was always with me on duty. You know, I didn't make the rotas. Anyway, I'd had enough of his sob story by then, so I picked up my bag and went to leave the office. He told me that I didn't need to leave and asked me to stay for another hour. I told him I was going home, and he told me that I wasn't. He thrust his hand up my skirt, grabbing at my underwear, trying to rip them from me, so I kneed him where it hurts, and he threw up all over me. He has never forgiven me.

"After that, he made my life hell, telling everyone that I had made a pass at him and that I was the reason why he and his wife split up. They believed him rather than me, so I left the force.

"Trouble is, I alleged that he had done it before to others, which didn't fare well with him. Now he is in a position of power. I think the past has come back to haunt me."

"Not quite, Rosemary," said Peter with a grin on his face. "Reception tells me that he received a call from the Home Office just now, telling him to release you with immediate effect. His exact words to me were to 'Get rid of her now. The woman's not to be detained'. You have friends in high places, Rosemary."

"Believe me when I tell you that this is not the last I have heard from him." She turned to face Robert, but he had disappeared. "Where's Robert?"

Robert emerged from the doorway of the courthouse. "Rose, you'll stay with me tonight. I have asked Andrew to put a watch on your flat. Not a word, please Peter."

"Not a word from me," the DCI replied, and they bid farewell.

Chapter 20

Rosemary and Robert were both silent in the taxi until it turned into Tudor Rose Caravan Park, just outside the town of Peacehaven.

"This is me," Robert said, pointing to the mobile home, surrounded by flowerpots. "You are one of the few people who know that I live here."

Rosemary smiled at him. "You are always full of surprises Robert."

He paid the taxi driver and led her to the door. "It is quite a humble abode, but it does me for what I need," said Robert, looking to Rosemary for acceptance.

"It's perfect," she replied. "You like flowers, Robert," she said, looking at the vast range of flowerpots along the side of the home. "The fragrance is gorgeous, and the colours are beautiful. I did not expect this of you."

Robert laughed. "Come in and I shall cook us a late breakfast and you can tell me all about Manville's Farm."

He opened the door into the small corridor and led her into the lounge.

"I'm sorry I couldn't take the calls when you needed me, Rose. It won't happen again."

Rosemary faced him.

"It's okay, Robert."

"It's not, Rose. I let my wife down by being late to meet her, and she died because of me. I promised myself, and to her at her funeral for that matter, that I wouldn't be late or leave a friend or colleague in the lurch ever again."

"I'm okay Robert, and you do look after me, for which I'm grateful."

She stepped forward to face him and putting her arms around his neck, pulled him close and kissed him slightly on the cheek. "Thanks Robert, for letting me stay here."

His eyes focused upon Jenny's photo on the wall behind Rosemary. Jenny's eyes seemed to be smiling back at him.

Rosemary let go and seeing his eyes were focused on the portrait photo of his late wife said, "She was beautiful, Robert."

"More than anyone will ever know."

He thought about his and Jenny's time together, when he used to pull her into his body and relish her warmth against his, her deep slow breathing rhythmically like his. What he would give for just one more day.

Rosemary saw the sadness in his eyes and thought about her short time with her own husband.

"Let me show you around and then I'll get you something to eat. You must be famished."

Rosemary nodded. "Thank you."

Rosemary found the home surprisingly spacious, its triple aspect lounge/diner faced south and looked over the English Channel from the home's elevated position, the large kitchen, as she was expecting, after his blitz on hers, was clean and well laid out, and the three double bedrooms were kitted out with folded towels at the foot of the guests' bedrooms, just like an upmarket hotel.

"This is your room, Rose, and there's an en-suite through there," he gestured, pointing to the satin white panelled door, on the far side of the room, beyond the double bed which was covered in a white linen duvet. Cut flowers were displayed in a tulip-shaped glass vase on top of the drawer unit in front of the partially opened window, wafting their summer scent through the room. "I'll leave you to freshen up whilst I make us some brunch." He left, closing the door behind him, leaving her alone.

Rosemary scouted the bedroom and en-suite, opening and shutting wardrobe doors and drawers, to find empty cupboards, then sat on the side of the bed, running her right hand over the neatly pressed duvet cover. She grabbed the pillow, the pillowcase again crisp white and burying her head in the soft duck feathered pillows, she smelt the fresh linen cover. She was tired. She replaced the pillow at the top of the bed, kicked her trainers off, lifted and swung her legs onto the bed and laid her head down on the pillow and closed her eyes.

Rosemary awoke to the 'choking call' sound of seagulls. Her eyes opened, then darted left and right as she tried to recognise her surroundings. She heard a door close outside of the room, and she listened to the unfamiliar noises in the new surroundings. She cautiously swung her legs off the bed and slipped her feet into her trainers. She stood to see herself in the long mirror on the wardrobe door, dressed in her Adidas tracksuit top and jogging bottoms, then checked out the room around her. There were no pictures on the painted walls, just the vase of flowers in the window. The smell of the cut flowers filled her nostrils and she remembered that she was at Robert's place. She smiled to herself, as her thoughts focused on Robert; the man who she had been introduced to during a night out, and who later in the same week, had turned up at her first-floor office for the interview as a partner in her private investigators practice. She had immediately taken a liking to him and now thought of him as a trusted colleague, a friend and a confidant.

Rosemary emerged from her room into the corridor and smelt the unmistakable aroma of a roast beef dinner, and she immediately checked her watch; it was just after one o'clock. She reached the lounge-diner door and heard the sizzle of oven-ready roast potatoes, together with soft classical background music. Opening the door, she saw Robert serving the hot food on three plates.

Robert turned to see her standing at the doorway.

"Thought that you might be hungry, Rose."

He smiled, then he noted the look of shock on her face.

"Robert, I'm sorry," Rosemary said, "you were making brunch for me. I hope you didn't waste it on my account."

Robert patted his stomach.

"Nothing goes to waste here, Rose. Take a seat, lunch is ready."

She turned towards the dining table, it had been set for three and before Rosemary could ask, Robert said, "The DCI is joining us for lunch. He has more information on the fire at Manville's Farm."

****

Sitting at the table, Robert and Rosemary listened to the DCI's account of how Jean Manville had died, and the details of the statements which had been taken from the shopkeeper, Chloe, and her mother, Deborah Branning. They had all finished their plates of food when the DCI concluded, "They both maintain that you bought the flowers for Jean Manville and although there is no evidence of the transaction, both stories corroborate."

Rosemary shook her head in disbelief. "Why would they lie?" she asked them both, "I told Walker what had happened, but he wasn't prepared to listen, so I thought it best not to tell him about the recording."

"What recording?" Peter asked.

Robert started laughing as he cleared the empty plates from the table.

"Peter, you should know Rose better than that, she's a smart cookie and was far too good for the force."

Rosemary smiled at her partner's comment. "I recorded the conversation between Jean and myself."

"The wonders of technology, eh, Peter," remarked Robert, chuckling to himself.

"What's more," Rosemary continued, "I recorded the conversation I had with Deborah and her daughter, Chloe, too."

Rosemary took the mobile phone from her tracksuit bottoms pocket, placed it on the table and pressed play.

****

Walker leaned back in his executive leather chair and smiled smugly to himself.

At last, he had his chance to get Rosemary 'frigid' Chandler back for nearly ending his career, all that time ago.

That fucking bitch was gagging for it and she knew it, he thought, as he watched his young PA enter the room, her tight blouse struggling to hold in her large breasts. She swayed her hips across the room, walking towards him and as she reached the desk and leaned forward, she placed the cup and saucer of hot tea in front of him, taking deep breaths to accentuate her heaving breasts. He was mesmerised by her cleavage. He thanked her for the tea and watched as she turned around and swayed seductively out of his office, the tops of her stockings just visible between the split in the back of her figure-hugging skirt. He picked up the hot mug of tea, smiling to himself, thinking of the wild night that he was going to have with that dumb bitch, Chloe Branning. Unlike Rosemary Chandler, Chloe would succumb to his demands, however he chose to use her.

He placed the cup down on its saucer, grabbed his personal mobile and made the call.

"Mrs Branning, is everything ready for me tonight?"

He smiled at her reply.

"I shall be around after dark, so make sure that Chloe is ready for me, and I don't want her makeup smudged like it was last time."

He smiled at the response again.

"Oh, one more thing. Your statement: did you tell them everything?"

He was enjoying the answers given. "What about Chloe?"

He once again listened to her answer.

"Good. I shall make sure that Chloe gets that polka dot dress that she told you she wanted."

He ceased the call and once again thought of the evening ahead of him. *Tonight Chloe, you will be Rosemary*, he thought, as he grinned wickedly to himself, 'and then I will deal with you' he gestured pointing at the tape recording of Rosemary's interview with him earlier, placed on the desk in front of him.

Chapter 21

Rosemary was unable to etch from her mind the events over the last couple of days, as she sat on the wooden bench with Robert Fox, waiting for their target to emerge from the historic dockyard gates. The recording of her conversations played to Robert and the DCI the previous day had cemented that she was not responsible for Jean Manville's death.

Who then had murdered Jean? Was it the fact that Jean Manville had been telling the truth about her and the old headmaster? Was her murder to silence her from re-telling her account? Why had the Branning's lied to the police? What did they have to gain, or lose?

The murder investigation was firmly in the hands of the police, so Robert and Rosemary agreed that they would pursue another line of enquiry; finding Charlotte's remaining 'Heroes'.

The main roads circumnavigating the boundary wall to the Naval Base had been heaving with traffic since four-thirty that afternoon, the occupants of the vehicles jockeying for positions so that they could be the first out of Portsmouth.

On their arrival, Robert had thought that they had missed John Branning amongst the throng of men and women leaving the yard. They both agreed to wait for another hour, and at just before 6 pm, Rosemary spotted the lone figure flashing his Naval Base pass to the security personnel, as he exited Victory Gate directly in front of them.

"There's our man, Robert," she said, pointing towards the gate.

John Branning was tall and slim, with receding white hair. Dressed in a light grey thick woollen jumper, blue Levis jeans and white and black striped trainers, he crossed the street and went into the first public house on the seafront road.

"Fancy a drink, Rose?" asked Robert. She nodded.

They crossed the road and entered the old traditional pub. Robert quickly scanned the busy bar. Several of the patrons sitting at the bar turned towards the shaft of light beaming through the open doorway to see the newcomers enter and walk purposefully towards the crowded bar. Robert had spotted John Branning sitting at the table for four by the window, on his own with a half-empty pint glass of lager in front of him, and his duffle bag beside him on the old wooden bench seat.

The barman was quick to serve them both, and they strode over to where John Branning was sitting. Robert placed a pint of lager in front of Branning. John looked up, gave them both a smile and a thumb's up, appreciative of the free drink, and in his quiet voice said, "Don't tell me. You are reporters, right? The free drink is for information, I presume?"

"If you say so," Robert replied.

"May we join you?" Rosemary asked.

"It's a free country," Branning responded, offering them both the bench seat opposite.

"Were you expecting us?" Rosemary asked as they took their places opposite the middle-aged sailor.

"Not much happens in Plumpton nowadays, so when I hear about the murder of Mrs Manville, it spikes my interest somewhat."

"Mr Branning, or do we call you Captain?" Rosemary asked.

John let out a burst of laughter. "Captain? You have been talking to my dear mum. She does like to exaggerate. I'm the Ship's carpenter, and who might you be?"

A couple of the locals approached the table, having heard John Branning laugh. "Are these two bothering you, Branny?" asked the larger of the two men, in a thick Scottish accent.

"They're fine, Scotty, but thanks. See you tomorrow." John replied, raising his thumb.

Scotty fixed his eyes on Robert and Rosemary for a few seconds, checking them over, and then replied, "Aye, Branny." Scotty and his accomplice returned to the bar.

Rosemary leant forward and placed a business card on the table, next to John's drink, which he quickly scanned.

"Private Investigators. What do you want with me?"

"We are investigating the disappearance of Peter Dennett and we wanted your help," Rosemary said, deciding not to make mention that she was the last but one person who had seen Jean Manville alive.

"After fifty years. I don't see how I can help you unless, of course, you want my version of what my mother has told you."

"Why would we want your version, Mr Branning?" Robert asked.

"Good question and you can call me John," Branning replied, placing the empty glass to one side and picking up the full one. "My mum is only interested in one thing – herself; if there's money to be made or a deal to be done that benefits her, she'll make the most of it, then she'll screw everyone else" – John took a gulp of his lager and then continued – "She tells everyone that I am Captain of Victory, to make herself feel important, and then when I correct her on the rare occasions that I return home, she makes excuses for me to her friends. I go home to see Chloe rather than my mum. My sister has learning difficulties, as you've no doubt seen, so I take her small gifts when I visit because she doesn't get much in the way of presents or treats from her mum. She will sit with me for hours listening to the stories I tell her about my days at sea, and then when I go to leave, she grabs hold and asks me to stay. Believe me, if I could, I would, but going home for good is not an option for me. My time as a kid at home was not good."

"Is that why you joined the Navy, John?" Robert asked.

"Seen the world," he responded, "with true friends and colleagues, who have your back and who you can rely on."

Rosemary nodded. "Got that."

Rosemary sensed that John Branning was at home here, a loner perhaps, but he felt safe in his surroundings.

"So, what can I tell you about the old headmaster, other than what you already probably know? Let us start with the things that you both probably don't know."

Branning took another gulp of his lager.

"Well, although many will say he was a great man, a saviour of the school and a man loved by everyone in the village, I, and I am sure many of my old school pals, have a totally different perspective."

He took a gulp of his lager and placed it back on the table.

"Peter Dennett took great pleasure in having his way with us when he was headmaster of the school." Branning hesitated, then took another gulp of his lager.

"I, for one, am pleased he went missing when he did because he couldn't hurt me anymore."

Rosemary stared in disbelief at what Branning had just said.

He forced a smile at her and then continued.

"It's just one of those things that happens."

"That's exactly what Jean said," remarked Rosemary to Robert, and immediately regretted saying it in front of Branning.

"You've seen Jean, have you?" asked Branning. "The headmaster probably raped her, too. No one spoke about what he did, they were too frightened to. He was part of a group that took advantage of everyone else. They had money, power, and status."

"It's not meant to be like that, John. Children and their mums should be safe in their own home."

"I'm not after sympathy," Branning replied, "I'm happy to just tell the truth now, having heard about Jean's death. She looked out for me, you know, when I was a lad, just like her, Alan."

"What truth, John?" asked Rosemary.

"The truth about what happened to me years ago, and you and Chloe yesterday, at the hands of my mother."

"About me and Chloe?"

Branning nodded. "My mum thinks that she has total control over everyone, including my stepsister Chloe, but she doesn't. Chloe has a mobile phone, which I gave her a year ago, hidden away from our mum, that she contacts me on whenever she has the chance. She told me about what happened yesterday, about how you came into the shop, to buy flowers, having visited Jean beforehand, and how my narcissistic mother persuaded her to lie to the police about your involvement."

"When did she tell you this?" asked Rosemary.

"This morning, whilst she was delivering newspapers on her motorbike."

"I have seen her on her bike, all dressed in her leathers. She rides well, John."

"It's her only escape for now," Branning responded.

"For now, John?" asked Rosemary.

"It will be no surprise to anyone how Chloe does everything my mum tells her to."

"I have seen that; she's very attentive towards her," Rosemary acknowledged.

"Yes, she is. What are not so visible are the scars that Chloe bears under her clothes, from the beatings that she must endure from my mum."

"Can't you report your mother to the police, John?" Rosemary replied.

"I would if they would take any notice, but there are members of that group who are in senior positions, magistrates, police officers as well as parents of the children themselves."

Looking directly at Rosemary, Branning said, "I can take Chloe away from all the harm that she is suffering, but I need your help."

"How can we help, John?"

"I shall tell you all that you want to know about Peter Dennett if you can persuade your contacts in the police to take me seriously."

Branning took another gulp of lager.

"I want to stop my mum from hurting my sister, but Chloe would never forgive me for grassing on our mum, so I need you to talk to your contacts in the Police Force about what's been going on, but do not approach Walker."

"Chief Superintendent Raymond Walker?"

Branning nodded.

"Why not him, John?" asked Rosemary.

Branning grabbed his phone from his pocket, and scrolled his hand across the screen, then handed the phone to Rosemary.

"I'll let you see for yourself but take it outside first."

"Okay." Rosemary stood to go and Branning grabbed her arm.

"I would take Robert with you if I were you. Whilst you are outside, I will be getting myself another lager. Same for yourselves?"

"Please and thank you," said Rosemary. They both walked outside, crossed the road, and sat on the wooden bench opposite the pub.

Rosemary looked at the image of Chloe lying on the bed in a polka dot dress. She pressed play and the image sprang into life. They could both hear her mum's voice in the background. "Now do as he tells you, and don't forget, your name is not Chloe tonight, it's Rosemary."

They heard Chloe say, "Yes, mum," and then saw her body tense rigid as the back of a tall man came into view on the screen.

"You are mine tonight, Rosemary," he snarled.

Rosemary recognised the voice immediately. The nightmare memories of him clawing at her underwear came flooding back to her in an instant.

The naked man laid down on top of Chloe, forcing her hands above her head, tying them both to the bedhead.

"Please don't," cried out Chloe, to no avail, as they saw the dress being torn from her body.

Rosemary couldn't believe what she was hearing. "It's Walker, Robert!"

Chapter 22

"You shouldn't have to watch this, Rose," Robert said quietly to her, taking the iPhone from her and stopping the recording.

Rosemary took a couple of deep breaths. "Walker's a sociopath, who uses his position and his power over vulnerable people, to get his sordid way, just as he tried to with me."

"What do you want to do, Rose?" asked Robert.

"He ruined my career, my confidence, my distrust in men. I couldn't stop him preying on vulnerable women then, but I can now, Robert, with this."

"You're just going to walk into his Station…"

Rosemary looked directly ahead to the pub opposite, forcing herself to stem the tears welling in her eyes. "Robert! The man needs to be stopped, and John Branning wants our help to stop him from hurting his sister again."

"What about his mother, Rose?"

"She needs to be brought to book too."

"Is that what John wants, Rose?"

"His mother lets Walker abuse her own daughter, Robert. Whose side are you on?"

There was a moment's silence. Robert could feel Rose's anger rising to boiling point.

"I'm on your side Rose, and John's and Chloe's for that matter," he replied calmly, turning to look at her, his eyes not showing the pity he felt for them.

Rosemary turned her head and looked at the rugged faced man sitting next to her. Robert had gained more than her trust.

"I'm sorry Robert, it's just—"

Robert swung his arm around her shoulders and pulled her towards him, her head leaning on his chest. She closed her eyes tightly, wanting the moment to last forever. He gave her a tight squeeze, then let his arm loose and said, "Let's talk to John again, and then we'll set about dealing once and for all, with Chief Superintendent Walker."

Rosemary topped her head back, looking at Robert, who was now looking over to the pub. She wanted to plant a kiss on his cheek but thought better of it. "Let's see what John has to say first," she replied, and they both stood, and checking the busy road, took advantage of the gap in the traffic and crossed over to the opposite pavement and into the pub.

****

The leather-clad motorcyclist, hidden behind the bus shelter, astride her motorcycle, watched them as they entered through the pub's doors.

****

John was still seated at the same table, his pint glass refreshed, and two more lagers were placed ready for Robert and Rosemary.

John detected the change in both of their faces as they re-joined him at the table.

"I'm sorry you had to see the video," John said, looking directly at Rosemary. He could see from her red eyes that the video had affected her more than her partner. "Now you understand why I must take Chloe away."

"When did you discover that Chloe was being abused?" asked Rosemary.

"It was when I showed her how to use FaceTime on her phone a week ago. She had been complaining about me not seeing her, and so I showed her how we could talk and see each other on the phone. I remember her face appearing on the screen, she was so excited to tell me about her new leather jacket that my mother had bought her, so I asked her to show me. She turned the phone around to focus on the leather jacket hanging on the hook on the wall, next to the long mirror, talking to me about all the pockets for her phone, her camera, her pencils, and crayons. Nobody takes an interest in her, so they aren't aware that she is brilliant at art; I shall show you some of her drawings one day. Anyway, it wasn't the jacket that I was interested in, it was the reflection of her body in the mirror. There was bruising on her upper arms, wrists and ankles which looked like restraint marks, which I focused on. I told her to cover herself up. When she phoned me, she was only wearing her underwear. I remember us both laughing, because I dropped my phone and it fell to the floor, and she saw that I was wearing the Superman socks which she had bought me for my birthday earlier in the year.

"I remember telling her to cover up before she contacted me on FaceTime again. When I told her to do something, she always replied, 'Okay John, whatever you say.' I dropped into our conversation about the marks I had seen, so as not to frighten her, and her expression suddenly changed. After a long conversation, she told me how she played dressing and undressing games with 'mum's friends', and how sometimes my mother would strap her, face down on the bed, and then she would wait for the heavy men to lay on top of her. I asked her if they hurt her, and she told me that it did hurt a long time ago, but not now. I told her how to use the camera in video mode on the phone and where to place it in her bedroom, so she could show me what they did to her, the next time that it happened, to which she replied, 'Okay John, whatever you say.'" John bowed his head in shame, hiding his face in his hands. "I didn't know until she showed me the video," he said quietly.

"This isn't your fault John," said Rosemary, watching the man across the table from her, telling total strangers his story.

Robert saw that John's reaction triggered 'Scotty' and his mate to react. The two mariners walked towards the table, "Hey Branny, you okay mate?"

"We've just had to tell him some bad news," Robert explained, as they reached the table, both men with their fists clenched, ready for a fight.

"I wasn't talking to you, laddie," Scotty replied, "So keep it shut." Scotty pointed to Robert's mouth.

Robert could sense this wasn't going to end well unless he defused the situation. Rosemary beat him to it. "John has just heard some sad news about his mother," she explained, "and he'd like a moment with us, on his own please."

The two mariners stopped in their tracks, "I'm sorry, Branny", said Scotty. The other added, "If there's anything we can do?"

Scotty looked directly at Rosemary. "Sorry love, we are just looking after our own."

"He's lucky to have you looking out for him," Rosemary replied.

"It's okay, lads," Branning said, looking at them both with a soulful expression.

The mariners both nodded and returned to their seats at the bar, discussing the news.

"How long has this been going on for, John?" Rosemary asked, her hand now holding his across the table.

"Too long, I would imagine," John replied.

"And when was the video taken, John?" Robert asked.

"Last night. I received the video from Chloe this morning. I watched it, didn't know what to do at first, so came here for a drink first, and then you turned up. So, I am asking you to help me save Chloe. I had always thought that it was just me who was the pawn to my mother's abuse until I saw those bruises on Chloe's arms and legs, and now the video has confirmed that my mother hasn't changed at all."

Rosemary shook her head. "All this time and she hasn't said a thing to anyone?"

John shook his head. "It appears that we have all been duped by my mum's apparent frailty." Rosemary could see John's jaw tightening, his eyes stared straight through hers.

"I feel your anger and frustration John and we're sorry too," Rosemary replied.

"Here's the deal, John," announced Robert, wanting to bring closure. "We shall save Chloe for you. We do, however, want to know everything about Peter Dennett."

John nodded. "Agreed."

"Your mother tells me that she gave you your photo album when you left home to join the Navy. Have you still got it with you?" asked Rosemary.

"Do you mean the old scrapbook?"

"Yes, apparently there are photos of you when you were at school."

"Yeah, I got it somewhere. Why?"

"Just like to see it, let's call it part of the deal," Robert intervened.

"Okay. One thing though. My mum never gave me the scrapbook, she lashed out at me when I left home, struggled like mad to snatch it back, but it was the only thing she treasured, so I took it to hurt her badly. She's forever trying to persuade Chloe to get it back from me, but she's not having it."

"What about your mother, John?" Rosemary asked.

"She can go to hell," replied John.

****

The leather-clad motorcyclist had been listening to the conversation via the same device, which she had used when she listened to Rosemary and Jean Manville.

She picked out her iPhone and made a call. "I have another irritation that I would like you to take care of."

"When and where?" came the reply.

"Wait."

Out of the corner of her eye, she spotted a rotund traffic warden waddling towards her.

She continued. "Portsmouth, tomorrow. Must go now," the woman replied. She turned off the listening device, slipping it into the rucksack which was resting on the fuel tank. She zipped up the bag, slung it across her shoulders and tightened the straps before starting the bike with a loud roar.

As she weaved her powerful motorbike through the traffic, she planned on how and when John Branning would be meeting Jean Manville and Trevor Johnson, in hell.

Chapter 23

The Ford Galaxy pulled up at the kerbside, outside of the black entrance door to the block of flats, just as Robert finished the call to DCI Peter Jones. It was dark and the car's reflection from the streetlights cast a shadow on the glossy black door of the block.

Having left John Branning sitting in the pub on his own, Robert and Rosemary had contemplated their next move, when and who to tell about Chloe's abuse at the hands of her own mother and Rosemary's nemesis, Chief Superintendent Raymond Walker.

Rosemary knew that she had the opportunity to show those who had previously dismissed her cries for help that her assailant, Walker, was indeed a sexual predator. Proof had been granted to her and Robert by none other than one of the 'Heroes' they had been searching for in their quest to learn more about the old headmaster, Peter Dennett. John Branning had too suffered from sexual abuse from the two or more people who should have kept him safe: his mother, his headmaster, and others yet to be identified.

"How can a mother subject her children to such abhorrent abuse, Robert?" Rosemary asked.

"No one really knows what goes on behind closed doors. It's only when evidence like this comes to light that the real truth comes out, Rose," he replied, waving his phone, which had the video footage on it.

"I couldn't even begin to think of hurting my children, if I ever have them, that is," Rosemary said, "could you Robert?"

"Night Rose," he replied.

He was silent for a minute, and Rosemary could sense that he was deep in thought. "You okay, Robert?"

"Yes, fine Rose, just been a long day. See you tomorrow."

Rosemary acknowledged his cue. "See you tomorrow Robert and thank you for everything."

He nodded, and Rosemary got out of his car, shutting the door behind her. His car pulled away from the kerb. She watched as it turned sharply left into the next street and disappeared behind the construction site hoarding. Rosemary sensed Robert's change in mood; *had she hit a nerve again?* she thought, perhaps about the subject of children. She made a mental note to ask why she had upset him. As she opened the entrance door to the lobby, the passive infrared sensor detected her movement, illuminating the route to her third-floor flat.

Standing outside of her door to her flat, she fumbled for the key, then arrowed it into the lock, turning the lock a half turn, which disengaged the latch. Rosemary stopped, frozen to the spot, as she listened for movement from inside of the flat.

Someone's been here, she thought.

She always double-locked the door when she left the flat, but it wasn't double-locked now.

She held her breath, listening for anything out of the ordinary. Nothing. The usual noise of the loud television next door had ceased when the elderly partially deaf neighbour, who she had never met, had moved out.

She kept still, listening for anything. There was no light coming from inside of the flat and everything was still. Rosemary had been standing still for too long, there was a click of the timer switch, and the corridor was suddenly plunged into darkness. She pushed her flat door ajar, extending her arm inside of the gap in the doorway, fumbling for the light switch. She felt two hands grab onto her wrist like a vice, pulling her into her flat, her head and shoulders smacking hard against the partially opened door, flinging the door open against the wall of the hallway with a loud thud. Her feet tripped over what she thought was someone else's foot and she fell face down onto the carpet, arms outstretched in front of her. The door slammed shut behind her, and then she cried out in pain as the assailant's knees slammed down onto her back, forcing the air from her lungs. She struggled to get free, but the heavy weight of somebody on her back made it almost impossible to breathe. She felt a cold ring of metal snap around her right wrist, then she felt a punch to her left kidney, and then the left arm was grabbed by the unknown assailant. Again, a ring of cold metal snapped around the left wrist, and she realised that she was being restrained in handcuffs. She felt a hand forcing her head into the deep pile carpet, her scream muffled by the long carpet fibres filling her mouth. Rosemary took in a breath and attempted to scream again, but a large powerful hand clamped around her mouth. She tried to bite the hand, but the hand-pulled her head back this time, her eyes opening wide to see a clear plastic bag being tucked under her chin and forced over her head. The hand across her mouth was taken away and she screamed again. She could feel the bag being tightened around her neck and for the first time, she knew she was about to die.

She breathed in deeply and held her breath. She felt the bag clinging to her face first and then around her lips, nausea sweeping over her. She could hold her breath no more, and as the air escaped from her mouth, she sensed it was likely to be her last. She took one last intake of breath from the remaining air left in the bag, causing the plastic to seal over her mouth. She cried out to herself, 'Mum', her thoughts of her and her mum when she was a child playing in the park, and then all at once, darkness.

****

Branning had searched his apartment as soon as he had returned, until he found the sepia-coloured scrapbook, then, wrapping it in brown paper packaging, printed the receiver's name and address clearly in the centre on the front. He turned the package over and in bold letters, printed, *from Derek, Trevor, Keith, Alan, and Me – THE TRUE HEROES.*

The concierge phoned the local dispatch rider, he knew well, as Branning had requested, and now seated at his desk at Number One, Portsmouth, instructed the motorcycle courier to deliver the brown paper package to its destination before midnight.

****

Robert had seen Andrew Braithwaite's men parked in a car when he stopped outside of the front door to the flats. Shortly after turning the corner, he stopped just out of sight from Rosemary's flat window and stepping out of the car, doubled back to the intelligence officer's car. They recognised him instantly, "Hey Robert, how are you doing?"

"Great chaps. Anything to report?"

They scrolled through the photos taken on the wide screen of their camera, "Usual subjects, except this one, Robert. He arrived about an hour ago and is still inside."

Robert studied the figure in the flat cap closely. "Zoom in on his face, can you, Ron?"

Robert saw the unmistakable features of Raymond Walker on the screen.

"Follow me now. I need your help, and I hope that we're not too late."

****

Chief Superintendent Raymond Walker had not heard Robert turn the key in the lock of the door behind him, whilst he sat astride Rosemary, but the bang of the door against the wall made his head snap round.

A steel toe-capped boot connected with his jaw with a loud crack, propelling his body onto Rosemary's body, then he was lifted by two pairs of hands and thrust through the hallway into the kitchen-diner. One of the officers returned and seeing Rosemary on the floor, dialled 999 for the ambulance.

Robert stared at his partner lying motionless, with a plastic bag covering her head for just a second, before his survival training kicked in. In two strides, he leapt along the hallway and knelt above her head, ripping off the plastic bag. She was motionless. Robert heard the emergency call being made, and moving to her left side, he pulled her over onto her back, scrambled over her body to the opposite side, to give himself more room, tipped her jaw back and grabbed her shoulder hard. "Rose." Nothing. Lowering his head down to her chest, he listened for the heartbeat, his eyes focusing on her head, for any signs of life. Nothing. He sat up, outstretched his arms over her chest and with his hands one on top of the other, he pushed down his weight on her sternum, then released. Then again, and again.

****

First, there was an overwhelming feeling of nausea, then the involuntary rush of vomit projecting from her mouth, then the sudden intake of breath burning her empty lungs with such intensity. She could suddenly feel the powerful pressure crushing the centre of her chest, forcing the air out of her lungs again, causing her to wail like an urban red fox.

Her eyes opened, and through blurred vision, saw a figure directly over her. Rosemary threw up her cuffed hands in front of her and grabbed at the face, looking down at her, her fingernails clawing at and tearing away the skin. Powerful hands grabbed her wrists and held them tight.

"Rose, it's me, Robert," the familiar voice said, her wrists being held steadfast in a vice-like grip.

Her arms went limp, and Robert lowered them to her chest and let go. He stroked the top of her head, and lowering his head near to hers, he reassured her, "Rose, I'm here. You're safe now."

He continued stroking her head. "Rose, you're with me now, you're safe."

Rosemary saw Robert smiling at her. She smiled back. "Robert," she whispered.

He stroked her head again and then gently kissed her forehead. "Rest now, Rose, I'm going to get you out of here."

Her eyes closed.

****

Rosemary could hear female voices talking around her. Her eyes opened slightly to see people mingling around her.

"Hello, Miss Bennett. Rosemary."

"Where am I?"

"You are in hospital, Rosemary, you're quite safe. Your partner is here waiting to see you," replied the nurse directly beside her.

"Robert?" she enquired, turning her head to see the nurse smiling down at her.

"Yes, he's just outside."

"Can I see him?"

The nurse nodded.

"Oh wait. I must look like a mess. He can't see me like this," Rosemary replied, running her fingers through her hair.

"You look better than he does," the nurse replied, tittering to herself, drawing back the privacy curtain, to reveal Robert standing there, with a cup of water in one hand and a small bunch of flowers in the other.

Rosemary looked puzzled, then concerned. "What on earth happened to you?" she asked, her eyes focusing on his bloodied, deeply scarred face.

He smiled. "Remind me never to pick a fight with you, Rose. You are evil." He stepped forward, placed the cup on the bedside unit and placed the flowers on the bed.

"Robert, let me look at you."

She studied his face again. "Did I do that?" her face was horrified at the deep scratches around his eyes and on his cheeks.

Robert nodded.

"Really! Oh, Robert, I'm so sorry, how–why would I do that to you, Robert? Come here," she said, outstretching her arms.

"Dare I?" he replied, with a cheeky grin.

He lowered his head towards hers. She smelt his familiar aftershave as she hugged him, pulling him closer until his head touched hers, then whispered, "Love you."

Chapter 24

The news about the attempted murder of a young single female broke into the early morning television bulletin. It caught John Branning's attention, whilst he watched the sunrise from his south-east facing balcony, when the newscaster mentioned Rosemary Bennett's name. Turning his head back into the expansive lounge to face the wide-screen TV, he saw the photo of Rosemary Bennett on the left-hand side of the screen, and a photo of Chief Superintendent Raymond Walker on the right.

"Alexa, increase volume," he commanded. The newscaster's voice boomed out her commentary.

"Chief Superintendent Raymond Walker was arrested and charged with the attempted murder of a young private detective at her home, in the centre of Brighton last night, and shall be attending Brighton and Hove Magistrate's Court hearing this morning. He is also facing charges for the alleged sexual assault of a female shopkeeper, who cannot be named for legal reasons, possession of child pornography, and sexual assaults of three former female colleagues who have since left Surrey and Sussex Police Forces, in which he served, over the past twenty years."

****

Charlotte stood steadfast in the lounge of the Villiers Suite of the Grove Hotel, just outside of Watford, her eyes glued to the large wide-screen TV, watching the same news bulletin. She paced over to the connecting bedroom door.

"Kimberley, quickly. Come and see this," she called out, dressed in the Hotel's complimentary bathrobe.

Kimberley Honisett raced through from her bedroom to see Charlotte staring at the screen.

"Do you remember I told you about Rosemary Bennett, the private investigator?" she asked.

Kimberley nodded, focusing on the wide-screen television, wrapping her long strong arms around Charlotte's shoulders, pulling her tightly against her. "I remember you telling me."

"She was attacked in her home last night by Raymond Walker. Do you know him?" Charlotte asked.

"No, Charlotte. Why do you ask?" queried Kimberley.

"There's much more to this. I know there is," Charlotte replied.

"Let's see what they have to say," said Kimberley.

They both stood in silence, focusing on the news unfolding.

"A spokesperson has said that the Independent Police Complaints Commission has been informed of the arrest, and a further statement shall be released to the press later today," continued the newscaster, "our local crime reporter, Tracy Robbins is at the scene of the block of flats where the attempted murder of Rosemary Bennett took place."

"Thank you, Fiona," commenced the reporter, who was standing on the pavement, outside of the block of flats, along with other reporters from rival channels. "On the third floor of this block of flats behind me, the accused, Chief Superintendent Raymond Walker, entered the flat of a local private investigator, named Rosemary Bennett, at around nine-thirty yesterday evening waiting for his victim to return home from work. Miss Bennett returned to her home, where she was set upon by the off-duty senior police officer, who in an unprovoked attack, apparently knocked her to the floor and covered her head with a clear plastic bag, trying to suffocate his victim. One flat owner has said that she heard the victim screaming for help from inside of the flat, and when she saw three men storming into Miss Bennett's flat door, she called the police."

The shiny black front door opened and out stepped DCI Peter Jones, a familiar figure to Tracey Robbins.

From behind the cordon, she called out to the DCI. "DCI Jones, can I ask for your comment on how the investigation is going?"

The DCI strode over to the huddle of reporters. "There will be a press conference later today, but for now, there is nothing more to report. Excuse me." The DCI walked over to the waiting Police car.

"Who is leading the investigation, Inspector? Is it you?" shouted out another reporter.

"The IOPC has taken charge of this investigation, and so I ask you to wait for the press conference later today for further information," he replied to the reporters. He opened the rear door to the unmarked police car, slid into the rear seat, and the car sped away.

Charlotte muted the TV using the remote in her hand. "I'd like to find out how Rosemary is, Kimberley. She and her partner saved my life the other night. You won't mind, will you?"

Kimberley released her grip around Charlotte's shoulders and placing her hands on her hips, gently spun her around to face her, seeing the worry on Charlotte's face. She smiled reassuringly at Charlotte, and replied in a soft tone, "Why don't you call her this morning? You have her mobile number, and if she doesn't answer, leave a message on her office phone. I'm sure that she or someone else will call you back. Even better," Kimberley continued, "why don't we pop down to the florist in Watford town centre, after breakfast, and arrange for some flowers to be sent to her, with a card from you."

Charlotte smiled back at Kimberley, then wrapped her arms around her neck, placing her cheek against hers. "Yes, I'd like that, thank you. I always know you are there for me in a crisis."

Kimberley held her in her strong arms, and replied, "Anything for you, Charlotte. You were there for me in Poland, and I am forever grateful to you."

****

John Branning heard his phone ringing from inside of the flat. He raced into his bedroom and just as he reached it, the ringing stopped. The screen showed the missed call and then it pinged to inform him of a voicemail. He pressed the voicemail button and listened to the message from his sister, and choosing the last number dialled, he rang back.

It was answered on the first ring.

"John, it's Chloe. I am in a room with a nice policewoman. She has told me to phone you, John."

"You okay, Chloe?"

"Yes, John. I've had boiled eggs for breakfast with bread soldiers."

"That's lovely Chloe. Where is Mum, Chloe?"

"I don't know. Will you come and get me, John? Mum is not here, and I don't like it on my own, John."

John sensed that Chloe was frightened. "It's okay Chloe, everything is going to be okay. Can I talk to the police officer, Chloe?"

There was a short pause, and he could hear Chloe talking.

"Hello, John Branning?" asked a female to him over the phone.

"Yes. Who is this?" replied Branning.

"Hello John, my name is Constable Trish Berry. I'm here with your sister, Chloe, and she is quite safe. Your mother is not here at the moment; she is helping us with our enquiries."

"Promise me that you won't let my mother anywhere near her, Trish."

"As I have said, Mr Branning, your sister is quite safe with me."

It was a welcome relief. *Chloe is safe at last*, he thought.

The call to Chloe and the subsequent call to the police had lasted over an hour. He called into work to tell them that he wouldn't be in and spent the next two hours standing on his balcony watching the sun rise, as he made his plans to collect Chloe and bring her back to his place.

The mid-morning news bulletin brought him no further updates and reminded himself of his promise, he smiled to himself, grabbed his mobile phone out of his trouser pocket and chose Fox and Bennett's office number stored in his phone, dialled the number.

The phone rang three times and then the answer phone cut in. "Thank you for calling Fox and Bennett." It was Rosemary's voice greeting the caller. "We're sorry we cannot take your call at the moment, however, please leave a short message and your phone number, and we shall return your call as soon as we return."

"Hello Rosemary," John responded, "I have seen the news; I do hope that you are okay. Chloe's safe, thanks to you, and as I promised, I will tell you all I know about Peter Dennett."

****

The next day, Rosemary woke with a start. Her eyes sprang open, and in an instant, pain shot across her head from one temple to the other, momentarily increasing in intensity behind her eyes and she wanted to be sick. She took deep breaths to quell the nausea rising into her mouth.

She slowly raised her head to look beyond the front of the bed and saw the blue vertically pleated curtains surrounding her bed. Beyond, she could hear people chatting about the latest news and her name being mentioned in the conversation. She focused her attention on the exciting discussions, then suddenly, the curtains drew back.

"Good afternoon, Rosemary," a nurse greeted her, standing beside a white mobile medicine cabinet.

"Afternoon?" Rosemary responded.

"We thought we would let you sleep after your ordeal," she said, "and how are you feeling now?"

Rosemary raised her right hand to her forehead. "I have one hell of a banging headache," she said, "like someone is smashing a hammer against the inside of my skull."

"I'll get you something for the pain," the nurse replied, opening the lid of the cabinet, dispensing tablets into a beaker.

"Are you feeling sick at all?" asked the nurse.

Rosemary nodded.

"Any pain other than your head?"

Rosemary shook her head. "Why are the curtains drawn?"

The nurse handed her the beaker of painkillers and a cup of water. "We kept you in overnight, just to keep an eye on you to make sure you're okay. You've had quite an ordeal, and Miss Bennett, you are quite a celebrity now. We've had the press in, posing as all manner of relatives of yours, wanting to interview you about what happened yesterday, so we closed the curtains so nobody would disturb you."

Rosemary smarted at the pain inside of her head. "Celebrity?" she queried.

The nurse nodded. "Your face is all over the local and national news bulletins."

"Really?"

The nurse nodded again. "Surviving such a brutal attack by a man twice your size. I should think so. He's being treated in another ward and believe me; he doesn't look good at all."

"Here?" Rosemary replied, alarmed by the fact that he was close by.

"It's okay, Rosemary," the nurse responded, seeing the frightened patient, "he is under armed guard, and he certainly won't be able to leave his bed with the injuries he sustained, at the hands of the men who came to your rescue."

"One of them, your colleague, I think, has been telling us how courageous you've been. He told us that you and he are private investigators."

"Has he now?"

The nurse smiled, "Your colleague, he's got a soft spot for you, I think. Told us how you've put your detective agency prominently on the map. You may not have noticed, but he stayed by your bedside for most of the night, keeping an eye on you."

Rosemary was touched by the comment.

"Did he now?" she queried, a smile beaming across her face, "he's a sweetie, but don't you tell him I said that."

"He's quite a character, isn't he? When we gave you your painkiller last night, he asked if he could have some for his throat, face, and neck."

"Is Robert alright?" Rosemary enquired, concerned for him.

"His name's Robert, is it?" the nurse said, "I like Robert, he's nice."

Rosemary smiled at her.

"You are a very lucky woman" – she continued with a cheeky grin – "Do I sense that you two are an item, or is he a free spirit, I wonder?"

"From the glow on her cheeks, I think they are both an item," another nurse said, appearing from behind the first.

"Afraid not. He's single," responded Rosemary.

"Really? Ooh. You mean there's hope for me yet?" queried the second nurse, striking up the light banter between them all.

"What's this about him needing painkillers?" asked Rosemary to both nurses.

"Well," the first nurse replied, "Robert tells me he could have done with some after you dug your talons into his face at your flat, and boy, were they deep," she clarified.

Rosemary's mind raced back in time, but she couldn't remember clawing at him, she could only remember the plastic bag over her head, and she closed her eyes, as the headache returned with a vengeance.

"We should leave you to sleep," said the first nurse, "so get some rest." They closed the curtains and Rosemary lowered her head slowly to the pillow and closed her eyes.

She squeezed her eyes tightly, trying to force the returning nightmares from her head, but they flooded back in waves.

****

Sitting on one of the two leather couches which graced the entrance lobby to the private plush apartments of Number One, the tallest building in Portsmouth, the woman in the black motorcycle leathers peered over the local Southsea Lifestyle magazine, which she had been reading, to watch the national news bulletin about the attempted murder of Rosemary Bennett.

With her eyes, hidden behind mirrored glasses, focused on Rosemary's photo on the screen, she listened to the female reporter describe what had happened the previous evening, and how she'd survived the attempt on her life.

"You won't be so lucky with me, Rosemary Bennett," the woman in the motorcycle leathers said to herself, as she scrunched the magazine together in her glove-covered hands.

The 'bing' from the lift doors sounded as the doors opened and from behind the stainless-steel doors emerged John Branning, dressed in a tweed jacket over an open-neck shirt, jeans and loafers.

The woman immediately jumped to her feet, dropping the scrunched-up magazine on the glass-topped table, to the disgust of the concierge, and called over to Branning.

"John Branning?"

Branning looked over at the tall shapely woman dressed in black motorcycle leathers, her blonde hair tied back in a ponytail. His reflection was clearly visible in her mirrored glasses. "Yes?" he replied.

"I'm Becca. I'm sure Chloe mentioned me to you?" the woman replied.

"No, I don't think she has," Branning replied, taking a step towards her.

"We go out biking together," the woman responded quickly, "I need to talk to you in private about her."

The concierge saw the concern etch across John Branning's face. Branning had regularly spoken to the concierge about his visits to his sister, the bike he had bought her and solitary life with just her mum. The woman standing in his foyer had never featured in their conversations. "You okay, Mr Branning?" he asked, standing tall behind his desk.

The woman was clearly irritated by the concierge's interruption and turned to face him. "Do you mind? This is a private conversation."

"There's no need to talk to him like that," Branning scolded.

"I'm sorry John."

"Look, if you're after a story about the news bulletins and my sister, I have nothing to say, so leave me be," Branning stated, and walked through the revolving door out onto the footpath.

The woman watched him turn left towards the town centre and grabbing her black motorcycle helmet from the couch beside her, marched out of the lobby. The concierge saw her turn right and nestled back down in his comfy leatherette seat behind the reception desk and continued to read his novel.

The footsteps he heard a few minutes later, entering the lobby, alerted the concierge to someone's presence, and he looked up from his book to see the same shapely woman, this time with her black helmet on. He stood up to face the woman.

"You can't enter here with your helmet on. Can I ask you to take it off please?" he asked, pointing at the 'No Helmets to be Worn' sign on the top of the reception desk.

There was no answer, but he could sense that she was staring straight back at him.

"Look, I don't want any trouble, so just take your helmet off, or leave," he commanded.

He saw her right arm raise, and to his horror, the gun in her hand, now pointing straight at him, and without a word, there was a muffled thud.

He had no time to react, the bullet hit him firmly in the centre of his chest, launching him back into his chair.

The woman pulled the trigger once more, aiming at his chest again, then calmly lowering the gun to her side, stepped around the desk, lowered the concierge's body below the desk, pushed his chair under the desktop to hide the blood from the concierge's exit wounds, then took his pass card which was sitting on the desk, and made her way to the lift, where she inserted it into the card reader. The doors to the lift opened and she took the elevator to the top floor. Stepping out into the plush lobby, the shiny black helmet and smoked black visor hid her face from the discreetly placed CCTV. She smiled to herself as she stared directly into the camera.

There was only one door from the lobby, the one that led into John Branning's apartment, which she had no trouble entering with the passkey. Stepping into the hallway, she closed the door behind her and waited patiently for Branning to return.

Robert parked his car in the underground car park below Brighton Square and took the back stairs to Fox and Bennett's Office. From the front window, he looked down onto the narrow brick pathway of The Lanes, to see the throng of press reporters gathered against the opposite shop window, outside of the front entrance door to the office. The shop owner of the hat accessory outlet below was happily feeding the press with refreshments because they had become a magnet to all the shoppers passing by, whose curiosity then led them into her shop. The till hadn't stopped taking in money since it opened its doors at nine o'clock, the shop owner, Tegan, had told him on the phone earlier when she had enquired about the press outside her window. She had relished in her three minutes of fame being photographed and interviewed by the reporters about her now-famous detective agency neighbours – Fox and Bennett.

He turned to the wall-to-wall magnetic whiteboard, half of which was covered in photos of Peter Dennett, the old headmaster, Charlotte Embling and the five schoolboy's photos, all but Derek's current profile photos below, and underneath them, all of their current legends.

Robert admired the way in which Rosemary organised her side of the office, compared to his, which was stacked full of papers. The red blinking light on the answerphone caught his eye on the side of Rosemary's desk. Stepping closer, he saw that the phone had received twenty-three messages. He pressed the play button and listened. "Hello Rosemary, it's Tracey Jones from BBC Sussex. Hope you're feeling better after your ordeal. How about an exclusive on what happened last night? You'd be doing me a favour and be glad to help you with your next case. Call me, you've got my number." Robert saved the message.

The beep signalled the end of the message and the second began to play. *Another bloody reporter*, Robert thought, rolling his eyes to the ceiling. He continued to listen to the numerous messages from the local rags and national tabloids, promising her substantial sums of money for exclusive interviews, making notes on the calls received, ready to discuss with Rosemary when he visited her later in the day.

It was the twentieth message that grabbed his interest. It was from John Branning. He grabbed the phone, dialled John Branning's number, and listened to his recorded greeting. "John, it's Robert Fox," he replied, "thanks for your concern about Rosemary. She's doing well and with any luck, she will be out of hospital soon. It would be great to meet up with you. Rose will be resting over the next few days, but I can meet you tomorrow morning if you'd like. Perhaps you can give me a tour of HMS Victory whilst we chat about Peter Dennett. Call me on the number Rose gave you yesterday. Bye for now."

****

Standing beside the sideboard in John Branning's apartment, the woman stood listening to the message being recorded on Branning's answerphone. "I'm afraid that John Branning will not be meeting you tomorrow, Mr Fox."

Chapter 25

The queue for the car park at the Royal Sussex County Hospital extended beyond the entrance doors to the wards on Level Six of the Millennium Wing building. Robert was minding his own business, waiting patiently in his trusty Ford Galaxy, tapping his fingers on the steering wheel to the music from the radio, when there was a tap on the nearside front window. Rosemary's radiant smile made him laugh out loud, and he jabbed the button on the dashboard to release the central locking. Rosemary pulled open the door and jumped in.

"I am glad to see you, Robert. Thanks for coming to collect me. I am really grateful."

"Great to see that you're better, Rose. We're both going to stay at The Stables until the press gives us some space. They're like a committee of vultures around the office and at your place, all waiting for their exclusives."

The car in front of Robert's moved forward a few metres, so Robert took the opportunity to swing the car around, and leaving the queue behind him, drove out of the hospital grounds, and made for Southwick.

"Thought I'd give Tracey, from BBC Sussex, a call on the way, she's meeting us there. She's a good friend of yours, I hear."

"We went to school together, Robert. She stood by me during the sexual assault enquiry, and she was instrumental in me starting out on my own," replied Rosemary. "Thanks for calling her, Robert. I owe her one."

"We had a long discussion on the phone, and she told me how she helped you back then," Robert remarked, "all I can advise you is to be careful; she's still a reporter, Rose."

"She's one of the good ones, Robert. I know you don't like them, but she, especially, can be useful to us, and so I give her the inside stories when I can."

"If she's that good, Rose, why isn't she with the Nationals?"

"She's had plenty of offers, Robert, but for reasons only known to her, she stayed in Sussex. The viewers like and trust her, as I've said, she's one of the good ones."

There was silence for more time than Robert cared for.

"Those drugs they gave you were powerful—" he began.

"They make you say all kinds of things," Rosemary replied, looking over to him.

"Sure do, Rose. Make you say the most unusual things," he replied, then laughed.

"Robert, look what I was meaning to say was—"

"Thank you?" he interrupted.

"Exactly," she replied, relieved at his reply.

"You are welcome, Rose."

Robert glanced over, their eyes met, and they both smiled, then he changed the conversation.

"John Branning wants to talk to us," Robert began, "he left a message on the answerphone saying that he wants to tell us everything he knows about Peter Dennett."

"Is he alive, Robert?"

"He didn't say that, so I said I'd meet him tomorrow in Portsmouth. Thought you should rest up, so I said I'd meet him alone."

"I'd like to come, Robert."

"Thought you wouldn't want to miss the opportunity, Rose. All I'm going to say is if you're well enough, we'll start out early and see what he has to say."

"Thanks Robert."

As he turned into the drive of Chalk Hill Riding Stables, Stewart and Marcia were waiting outside to greet them.

****

Robert and Rosemary were sitting in the conservatory admiring the sunset go down over the Downs when Stewart appeared in the doorway, with the BBC reporter by his side.

"I'll leave you three alone to talk," he said.

"Thanks, Stewart," Robert replied.

The door closed and Robert ushered Tracey to the settee next to Rosemary, who stood to greet her.

"How are you feeling now, Rosemary?" Tracey asked.

"Sore," Rosemary replied, "more my pride rather than pain, I think."

"It's been ten years since he last assaulted you, Rosemary. What on earth was he thinking?"

"All I remember was him shouting at me about his father before I passed out."

"Do you know why?"

Rosemary shook her head.

"You managed to lose the other reporters, I see," Robert observed, checking the drive for unexpected visitors.

"You are yesterday's news, Robert," Tracey began, "there's been a murder in Portsmouth, where it's been reported that a man had been strapped to a chair and tortured before they killed him. The news is about to break out on all the news channels."

"They?" Rosemary asked.

"It looks like the assailant was a woman dressed in motorcycle leathers. Whether she was working alone is not clear. There is no immediate motive, however, he works on the Naval Base, a middle-aged man named John Branning."

Neither Robert nor Rosemary said a word about Branning to the news reporter but told her about the ordeal that Rosemary had suffered at the hands of Raymond Walker.

Having waved goodbye to Tracey Jones, as she left the Stables, Rosemary turned to Robert and said, "Looks like we shall not be meeting John Branning tomorrow, but let's try to get our hands on his photo album."

****

Rosemary had woken up the next morning, at five, as the early morning sun rose, shining its warm rays on the east side of the Chalk Hills Farmhouse. Now, an hour later, she was standing in the shower, the hot water splashing onto her body couldn't stop the shiver that ran down her spine.

She'd had a troubled night's sleep following her discussions with Tracey Jones, initially recollecting the horror of her ordeals at the hands of Raymond Walker, the night before last.

John Branning, their most promising witness so far, had indeed been tortured and then murdered in his own flat. Following Tracey's tip-off, the news had broken nationwide, but none had got wind of how he was tortured. DCI Peter Jones had told Robert that Branning had been tied to a chair, his fingernails and toenails removed and finally shot in the centre of his forehead; the graphic information being kept under wraps from the press at the behest of the criminal enforcement agencies.

Rosemary thought about the murders of Trevor Johnson and his wife, Louise, the attack on Charlotte, the murder of Jean Manville at the farm and now John Branning. Who was this woman in the black motorcycle leathers?

Rosemary had caught a glimpse of the woman at Charlotte's home, and Robert was convinced that there was a connection with the Johnson's deaths too.

The question was, why? Had the Heroes something to tell her about their old headmaster, or had they seen something that they shouldn't have in 1968? The headmaster was not the saint or saviour that he had made himself out to be.

More to the point, who was the leather-clad woman, and who was to be her her next victim? Rosemary confirmed to herself that there were only three remaining to choose from, Charlotte, Keith Wilton who was now Kimberley Honisett, and Alan Field, who had gone off-grid and was nowhere to be found.

What was common amongst them all? She had made a list and added commonalities to it in the middle of the night in between the restless bouts of sleep and now the list was replaying in her mind.

"Fresh air; that's what I need," she said to herself. She turned off the steaming hot shower, and towelled herself dry, then donned the soft-fleeced dressing gown which had been hung on the hook on the door.

Opening the door of the en-suite, Rosemary's eyes scanned the large bedroom to see an array of oil paintings around the room of the Downs, the views out to sea from high up on the hills, spot lit by the sliver of sunshine coming through the curtains which covered the large window.

She paced over to it, drew back the curtains and took in the uninterrupted view of the fields of maze stretching up to the chalk hills of the Downs. She opened the lead-light casement window to let the warm, fresh air into the room. She watched Paulina and Robert pulling up in his Galaxy, both getting out and

Robert retrieving a large suitcase from the boot, handing it to Paulina, and then striding over towards Stewart, who was busy collecting eggs from the chicken house to her right.

The Farm was idyllic, quiet, and so picturesque, she fully appreciated why Robert spent a lot of his time here.

There was a knock on the door. She strode over and opened it to see Paulina, looking sheepish, holding various clothes on hangers in her left hand and a large suitcase on the floor beside her, on her right.

"Robert made me go with him to your flat to get you a change of clothes. As you can see, we didn't know what you'd like, so we brought nearly everything."

"So I see," replied Rosemary smiling broadly at Paulina.

"He is feeling guilty about invading your privacy, but he didn't want you going back there whilst it was still a mess having been trampled over and examined by the forensic teams," Paulina blurted out quickly, "he wanted me to say sorry to you, rather than he does it himself because he…well he's just Robert."

Rosemary laughed at the final comment. "Come in, Paulina. That is so kind of you both, I was dreading wearing the same clothes again."

Rosemary took the suitcase and ushered Paulina into the room. Paulina laid the clothes gently down on the unmade bed and then saw the ones Rosemary had been wearing the previous day.

"Are these the clothes?" Paulina stopped mid-sentence, fearing herself saying the wrong thing, but Rosemary finished it off.

"That I was wearing when Walker attacked me? Yes, they are."

"I'm sorry, Rose," responded Paulina, tears welling in her eyes, "I can't imagine what you went through. It must have been horrific."

"It's over now," Rosemary replied, placing the suitcase on the floor and stepping over to Paulina, wrapping her arms around her neck and hugging her tightly. She noted that Robert was not the only person to call her Rose.

"It's me that should be hugging you. Is there anything I can do?" asked Paulina.

Rosemary gently let go of Paulina and then palmed away her tears from her rosy cheeks.

"Well, you could help me choose the right clothing to wear today."

"Love to. After what you have been through, you should rest. Perhaps you'd like to join me for a walk around the stables. Robert has asked me to look after you whilst he is away."

"He's away?" Rosemary asked.

"He hasn't told me where he's going, just that he thinks that it's best for you to rest," replied Paulina, "that is why we brought you so many clothes, so you could rest here for the weekend."

At that moment, Robert appeared at the open door.

"Do you mind Robert? Rose isn't dressed yet," Paulina chastised him as she made for the door.

"Of course. Sorry, Paulina. Rose, call you later. I'm off to see a few people."

"Do you want me to come with you, Robert?"

"Rather you stayed here, Rose."

Rosemary nodded; her disappointment palpable.

"You'll be safe here, away from the press and anyone else for that matter," Robert continued.

"Off you go then," Paulina ordered, "we've got lots to talk about." Paulina closed the door and Robert stood outside, listening to them start up the conversation.

"So how well do you know Robert, Paulina?" Rosemary asked.

"Oh, loads. Where do I start?" she said in a loud voice, then quickly swung the door open to see Robert standing there, shaking his head.

"Haven't you got somewhere to be, Robert? This is a girls' only chat, so be off. Scoot," she said jokingly, as she closed the door on him again.

"Robert has been a close friend of the family ever since I was a child," he heard Paulina saying to Rosemary, shook his head and walked downstairs and out of the front door.

****

The shapely leather-clad woman punched the number into her mobile.

On the third ring, a husky voice answered with a simple, "Yes."

"John Branning is dead," the leather-clad woman replied.

"I've seen the news. And the information that I required?" the voice enquired.

"He tells me that he wasn't there, and he hasn't got the envelope, and believe me, he would have told me, if he had," replied the woman, sitting astride her beloved Yamaha FRJ1300.

"I am in no doubt that he would. Your methods of extracting information have been extremely useful so far," came the response, the voice sounding impressed. "Did you obtain anything else from him?"

"He spoke to his school friend Alan yesterday, apparently. I have a phone number and an address up north where he can be found, from a contact I have at MI5. I'm on my way now," replied the woman, depressing the push start on the handle of the motorbike.

"I need that information, no matter what it costs," came the response.

"Have I failed you yet?" the leather-clad woman replied.

"No! I didn't say that you had," came the reply.

"And I won't let you down, not like your mother did." She heard the phone go dead, so she slid the iPhone into the zipped pocket of her jacket, revved the motorbike's engine, and selecting the gear, roared away.

****

Rosemary tilted her head back, embracing the warm sun on her face, as she leaned against the bonnet of Pauline's new Audi.

"Do you fancy a drive?" Rosemary asked, "The Lanes in Brighton was what I had in mind. Quirky shops, nice hat accessory store, and how about a meal at the Ivy in the Lanes? Be back before Robert returns tonight, what do you say?"

"Never been to the Ivy," replied Paulina.

"Ready when you are."

Chapter 26

Robert sat outside of the café in the park. He had walked twice around the shingle-covered path checking available entry and exit points, and the familiar faces of the afternoon Sunday walkers, in advance of his meeting with Andrew Braithwaite, prior to occupying a prime position on the stone patio. He placed the book he had brought with him on the table and turned the pages until he reached the book-marked page, tilted the book up slightly, and tipped his head forward as if he were reading 'The Da Vinci Code' novel.

He clocked a dark-haired, middle-aged man entering the Park, walking cautiously towards the Café, from the south entrance, immediately to his left. The man wore a pleated brown jacket, black jeans and scuffed black shoes. The man stopped at the serving counter, scanned the area of the park quickly, then bought two teas and hovered a little too long, for Robert's liking, by the corner of the timber cladding building, adjacent to the Café. A couple left the table near to him and the man sat in one of the chairs facing east.

Robert spotted Andrew entering the Park from the southeast entrance, as did the middle-aged man. Robert saw the shift of the man's body in his seat having spotted Andrew, so Robert took the phone from his jacket pocket and punching in a text, pushed send, then placed the phone face up on the table, next to his book.

A couple of seconds later, the screen lit up and Robert read the incoming text. He placed the phone back in his pocket and refocused on the book.

As Andrew drew closer to the Café, Robert saw the man shifting uneasily in his seat, as he scanned the area around him.

Robert sat still as Andrew passed him by, stopping at the next table. On cue, Robert turned in his chair to face them both. "Morning Andrew."

"Hello Robert, I thought it would be appropriate for you and Alan Field to meet in person,"

Before Alan could respond, Andrew placed his hand on Alan's shoulder for reassurance.

"Robert is on our side Alan, he is here because he can help you, and by the same token, you may well be able to assist him," Andrew confirmed.

"You are a hard man to find Alan," Robert started, "how did you and Andrew meet?"

Alan looked over to Andrew, again for reassurance, and Andrew nodded in affirmation.

"I called the police 0800 number last week after I heard about the murder of Trevor and his wife, Louise. I was told to go to the nearest Police station."

Alan was interrupted by the thunderous roar of a motorbike. Robert saw the panic in Alan's face, his red cheeks turning ashen.

"It's okay, Alan, you are safe with us," Andrew said to him to reassure him.

"I'm not safe anywhere," he said to Andrew, "I need to get away from here and then we can talk."

"Your car is close by, isn't it, Robert?" Andrew asked.

Robert nodded.

"Let's go, shall we?" suggested Robert. He rose from the chair, as did Andrew.

Alan looked at them in turn as he stood, then asked, "Where are we going?"

"A safe house," replied Robert.

Robert and Andrew flanked Alan on either side as they walked to Robert's Ford Galaxy.

Opening the rear door, Alan and Andrew climbed into the back seat, Robert closing it behind them, hiding their faces behind the privacy glass.

The two passengers watched Robert walk back to the café, stopping next to the leather-clad motorcyclist, patting them on the back, then returning to the car. Robert climbed into the driver's seat, started the engine, and engaging first gear, drove out of the park.

"I know I shouldn't ask Robert, but who is your contact in the leathers?" asked Andrew.

"Someone who is watching our backs, Andrew," Robert replied, as he cut into the traffic on the coast road, heading towards Eastbourne.

Robert saw Alan whisper to Andrew and registered the concern on Alan's face.

"The motorcycle bothered you, Alan. I saw your reaction at the café when you heard the engine," Robert said, interrupting Alan's whispers to Andrew.

"It's the noise of the motorcycle, and yes, it did bother me. It reminded me of last week. There was something not right. Perhaps I am overthinking things, but when I left Debbie's in Timsbury a few days ago, I saw a motorcycle roar up to the front door of the house, just as I was leaving. What was unusual was that the rider didn't remove their helmet when they walked into the house. I should have turned around just to go and see who it was, you know, just to satisfy my curiosity, but I didn't want to miss the train to Paddington."

"They didn't see you?" Robert enquired.

"I don't think so. I heard the motorbike first, then saw it turn into the drive, and stop immediately outside of the front door. The rider got off, took a small black bag out of the side pannier and walked up to the door. They didn't knock, they just walked in. I was in plain sight, the taxi had reversed into the driveway, ready for me, and as I was getting into it, the motorbike turned into the drive, rode straight past the taxi, and stopped. I don't think the rider would have recognised me from the corporate photos; I had previously shaved off my beard and Debbie had coloured my hair."

"The rider would have been looking for a redhead with a beard, then Alan," Robert confirmed.

"How do you know?"

"My partner showed me the photo she took of you on the front cover of the New Scientist which your mother had on her sideboard."

"Did your partner meet my mother, Robert?"

"She did. She spent the afternoon with her, Alan. How do you know the rider was looking for you?" asked Robert.

"Because when I got to Paddington, I went straight to Trevor's office to pick up an envelope from him that he wanted me to keep safe, I used the receptionist's phone to call Debbie, but there was no answer. I rang a second time from Trevor's office about ten minutes after that, and a policeman answered. He wanted my name, but I put the phone down. I told Trevor what had happened. Then a few days later, Trevor is murdered, along with his wife. Now my mother has been murdered. It is all such a mess, and all because—" Alan fell silent.

"Do you know what the envelope contained, Alan?"

"No, he just told me to take it to John, or Rosemary Chandler."

Robert stared into the rear-view mirror at his passenger's face, then at Andrew's.

"Did you know about this, Andrew?" Robert asked.

"Yes, I did Robert, late last night, mind, and thought it better that I came to you first-hand, and that's why I wanted to meet on our own, just you, me and Alan."

Alan picked up on the comment and asked, "Do you know Rosemary Chandler?"

"Yes, I do."

"Well, I've never heard of her, so I took it to John's apartment in Portsmouth a couple of days ago, but he wasn't there."

"Where's the envelope now?"

"I haven't got it, but it's safe."

"Where is it, Alan?"

"If I tell you, can you guarantee my safety?"

"Alan, you came to us, so we'd be grateful for your cooperation," Robert replied.

"I asked the Police for help, but I was told to go to the nearest police station and ask for Robert Fox."

"DCI Jones used your name, Robert, because we were worried that Alan would be placed in the wrong hands," said Braithwaite, interrupting Alan's recount.

Robert raised his eyebrows.

"They told me there was no Robert Fox at the station. I told them who I was, and they insisted that there was no one of that name at the station and suggested that I call this number, from the call box in the lobby."

He held up a note with the number on it.

"So, I did, and they told me to wait at the corner of the building by the flower stall. I did as I was told. Next thing I know is that I'm being bundled into the back of a van, a hood forced over my head and my wrists and ankles tied together, brought to a park and then instructed to meet this man in the photo."

Alan held up a photo of Andrew Braithwaite.

"When they released me from the van, the same man who unhooded me, apologised for the way I'd been treated, but said it was for my own good, then told me to do exactly as he said. What choice did I have?"

"We needed to be sure you were who you said you were, and once confirmed, that you were safe and that nobody followed you," Andrew responded.

"So why bring me here?"

"We have our reasons and believe me when I say it was the best option. You have nothing to fear. We're here to protect you."

"From what exactly," Alan replied, "you didn't protect my mother."

"We didn't know that your mother was in danger."

"Who killed her?"

"We don't know, neither do the police. That's why we need as much information as we can from you, and quickly, so we can do our job."

"What job is that exactly?"

Braithwaite intervened, "Defending the national security of this country, and you may play a crucial part in this, so please, we'd like your help, and you can start by telling us where the envelope is."

"It's with the only other person I trust; Keith."

"How did Trevor get hold of the envelope in the first place?"

Alan replied, "He was given it by our old teacher, Miss Embling."

Chapter 27

Charlotte sat on the stone slab seating, in the centre of Watford's shopping precinct, beside Kimberley, eating the takeaway sandwiches in the bright midday sun. They both sat in silence, watching the throng of shoppers darting in all directions, from shop to shop, carrying their array of purchases.

Charlotte's time with Kimberley was precious and they both knew it because, in two weeks' time, Kimberley would be starting her European tour of famous concert halls with the BBC orchestra, playing her famous piano renditions to her many admirers.

Charlotte so wanted to be at her side, listening to her play in the world's most famous music halls, but she knew her ageing body would never put up with the stresses and strains of hours of travelling between each of the venues.

Charlotte knew that Kimberley was dreading the next six months they would spend apart as much as she was and that what she was about to ask would hurt her, but she had to know. She stared straight ahead, not looking at Kimberley, and broke the silence between them.

"Do you remember when you all used to tell me about the spacemen?"

"I do," replied Kimberley, as she turned her head to look at her former teacher. "Why do you ask?"

Charlotte turned her head, and her eyes met the gaze of Kimberley, tears forming in her eyes. "When Derek died in my arms, his last words to me were, 'the spacemen', and I, forever, keep seeing him lying in my arms in my sleep, it gives me nightmares. It always haunts me when the image, of yours and Alan's, Trevor's and John's faces looking down at me that day, suddenly fills my mind."

"This image, is it on your mind now?" asked Kimberley.

"I'm sorry Kimberley, yes, it is, I just can't erase that moment in time. I never have done truthfully, it's just more vivid now. You have never told me about 'the spacemen' Kimberley, or why they frightened you all so much."

"They were frightening, Charlotte. We were just seven years old. I wasn't one for the adventures, really, but Derek certainly was, and I would go with him because he and I spent many of the evenings playing at my house. After all, his mother and father were always working on their farm. They never had time for him, Charlotte."

"So where do the spacemen fit into all of this?" Charlotte asked.

"It's a long story, Charlotte."

"I'd like to know, Kimberley, and I have been wanting to know about them for a long time, and this may be my last chance to ask."

"What do you mean, your last chance?" questioned Kimberley, as she reached over and took her hand in hers. "You're not leaving anytime soon, are you, Charlotte?"

"Not if I can help it, Kimberley. I just want these nightmares to go away. You understand me, don't you?"

Kimberley nodded. She reached over with her other hand and cupped Charlotte's hand with both of hers.

"Are you ill, Charlotte? Is there something you're not telling me?"

"Nothing for you to worry about. I just want to know why Derek died, the way he did."

"Alright then, let me begin from when we first saw them. Derek first told me about them when we were playing in my bedroom. We were dressing up in my mother's clothes, when I saw a cut under his arm," Kimberley said as she lifted Charlotte's hand above her head and traced the location of the cut by running her finger under Charlotte's arm, then placed it back in Charlotte's lap again.

"I remember him showing me," Charlotte replied.

"He showed you, Charlotte?" Kimberley quizzed, "he never told me that he had shown it to anyone else, and besides, it was bandaged up."

"I know. He asked me if I could redo the bandage one day."

Kimberley looked puzzled. "He told me that he never showed anyone else, except his mother, father and me."

"I was his teacher, Kimberley. He, like you, told me lots of things, which I have never told anyone else. You do understand that, don't you?" Charlotte asked.

"Of course, sorry," replied Kimberley. "Anyway, he told me that his parents had forbidden him to visit the old barn beyond the dense thicket on the farm, but he went there one evening after he left my house."

He told me first, then Trevor, John, and Alan, about the large shiny caravans all parked inside the barn, the doorways all joined together by corridors made from metal frames, covered in tarpaulin. He told us that he had seen the workmen putting up the tunnels and that was the first night that he saw one of the spacemen. He told me that he saw him standing in the doorway of one of the caravans, surrounded by a bright white light. The spacesuit was bright yellow, even down to his boots, but his face was hidden behind a fogged-up mask. Derek was so scared, he told me that he ran home to tell his parents, and on the way, he tripped over a stone and fell onto a broken steel fence post. Luckily, it only slashed his skin under his arm.

"His mother smacked him hard and made him promise to her that he would not say a word. I remember that I had to calm him down when he first told me because he was hyperventilating, so I rubbed his back and then held him tightly in my arms. I couldn't stop him from crying for a long time, Charlotte. He eventually calmed down and he showed me the bruising on his bottom, where he'd been smacked so hard. I think that must have been the only time that he was punished like that because he didn't complain again."

Charlotte cast her mind back, remembering when she received a handwritten letter from his mother, excusing him from P.E. for a couple of weeks, and now she realised why.

"He made me, John, Trevor and Alan promise not to tell anyone," Kimberley continued. "He had said that he didn't want another beating from his mother, and that was what had been promised to him if he told anyone about the barn. We all promised. We did all agree, though, that we would sneak up to the barn and investigate what was going on. When we all regularly visited the barn, we all saw the spacemen, and then one night, when we were crouching low, watching the comings and goings of the spacemen, we saw them carry out a large oil drum and then disappear back inside. We crawled up to the oil drum and looked inside. It smelt of petrol but was empty.

"We crawled back through the hole in the barn wall and waited to see what happened next. It was late evening and the sun had gone down. We heard a lot of shouting from inside of the caravans and then saw four spacemen emerge dangling large birds by their feet, their wings were splayed out, and they weren't alive. They dumped them in the oil drum, and it was set alight. The fire in the drum flared up and the heat from it caught one of the spacemen alight. The others ran to him, pushing him to the ground and smothering him with their hands, to extinguish the flames. They took off his hood and we instantly recognised the man behind the mask. It was Derek's father."

"So, Derek believed he was the son of a spaceman?"

"Yes. Derek's father didn't leave his wife, Charlotte, he was taken away."

"By whom?" asked Charlotte.

"No one knows. But he has never been seen again."

"What were they doing at the barn, do you know, Kimberley?"

"We had no idea then, but I have found out that they were developing vaccines for highly contagious viruses, such as Coronavirus."

"How did you find out?"

"Alan told me the other week when he called me out of the blue. He warned me to watch my back because the past had come back to haunt us, and then I received this."

Kimberley reached into the large carrier bag, pulling out a large, padded envelope. She dug her hand into the open flap and pulled out a brown paper envelope, which Charlotte immediately recognised.

"Oh no, Kimberley, I thought I'd got rid of that when I gave it to Trevor. Who gave it to you?"

Kimberley saw the fear in Charlotte's eyes.

"Alan sent it to me. I told him to send it to the Theatre. Why? What's in it?"

Charlotte looked at her watch, then dug her hand into her purse, retrieving a business card that had been handed to her just a few days ago.

"Come on, you'll be late for your own performance. On the way, we'll call into the post office. The package isn't safe in our hands," Charlotte continued, "but I know who to send it to, then I shall explain everything to you after the show."

Chapter 28

Paulina and Rosemary stepped out of the entrance to Ivy in the Lanes, Paulina strutting her model pose as Rosemary took her photo in front of the floral covered door surroundings.

"Thank you, Rose."

"It was lovely, wasn't it? We should get back before Robert finds us missing."

Paulina nodded.

"Is it alright with you if we pop into the office, Paulina? I just want to check on phone messages and the post."

"Yes, sure."

"We'll skirt around to the back entrance, just in case there's anybody we don't want to bump into at the front."

"Like whom?"

"The press or my landlord's wife."

****

The Ford Galaxy turned into the deep gravel-covered driveway and stopped outside the door behind a large black motorcycle.

Robert stepped from the car and opened the offside rear door to prise Alan Field out of the vehicle, to join him in front of the detached two-storey residence. He'd stopped his SUV on the seafront car park at the east end of Seaford, placed a hood over Alan's head, telling him it was for his own good. The three men travelled in silence to Robert's safe house, the journey extended to ensure that they weren't being followed.

He guided Alan into the house through the front door and into a large sitting room, where he removed his hood. Andrew followed, and behind him came a man he had seen in leather motorcycle gear at the Park earlier, talking with Robert.

"Where are we?" enquired Alan warily.

"You are in a safe place, Alan. The only people who know where we are, is Andrew, DCI Jones, and me," Robert replied.

"I'm not comfortable with this arrangement," Alan said, rubbing his eyes.

"You said yourself that you know that you are in danger, and we need to find out from who, and why? Here, we have time to find out all that you know and try to establish why you and your former school friends are being targeted, for one. Secondly, why you suddenly left your employer in Timsbury, and thirdly, what information you have which might be a threat to the national security of this country," explained Robert. Andrew and Peter stood staring at Alan in silence.

"I don't know if I can help. I just know that whatever is in the brown envelope which is with Keith, probably holds the answers. Trevor told me that they would go to any length to get their hands on it."

"Who's they?" asked Andrew.

"I don't know, but I will tell you now, whoever they are, undoubtedly killed Trevor and Louise, and my mother, in search of the envelope."

"What about John Branning?" asked Robert, "Do you think he died because of the envelope too?"

"John's dead?" asked Alan.

Robert nodded.

"No, he can't be. He knows nothing about what went on. He wasn't there when Keith, Derek and I were at the barn. His mother wouldn't let him out, so we left him at home."

"What didn't he know, Alan?" asked Robert.

"Derek died because we went to the barn on the night before he collapsed into Miss Embling's arms, in the school playground. We crawled through the hole in the side of the barn and saw the 'spacemen', as we called them, come out of an enclosure to the side of the caravans, leaving the door open. Derek wanted to see if his father was there, as he hadn't returned home for a month. I remember that he suddenly stood up and ran towards the enclosure; we were calling him, trying to get him to return, but he kept running and then he disappeared through the doorway. We couldn't leave him on his own, so we followed him and stood at the doorway. The room looked like an operating theatre in a hospital. In the middle of the room was a man who was lying in a metal tube, his head only visible on the outside."

"Sounds like he was in a mechanical respirator or Iron Lung, as they were commonly known as," remarked Andrew.

"He was," replied Alan, "he was thirsty and asked Derek to get him some water. We watched Derek grab a cup from the draining board nearby and fill it with water from the tap. We could hear Derek asking if the spacemen had taken his dad, only for the man to laugh. He asked for the water again and Derek gently tipped the cup slightly, letting the water trickle from it into the man's mouth.

"The man suddenly started coughing, the water in his mouth sprayed over Derek's face, which made Derek scream and he ran towards us. His scream was heard by the other men dressed in their yellow suits, because they all turned and faced us. We all turned on our heels to see the men in bright yellow hooded suits running towards us. We ran towards the hole in the barn's side, scrambling through it as quickly as we could and continued down the unmade road, the men chasing us. We outpaced them easily and they gave up the chase.

"We met John Branning running towards us, who told us that he had escaped from his bedroom, and then there were headlights fast approaching us. We turned to see how far away the men in suits were, but they had gone. My father's Land Rover pulled up and he was with John's mother, who was searching for him and us.

"They were so angry because we were all out so late, that they didn't want to hear what we had to say. I got my father's belt across the back of my legs when I got home, and I know the others received similar punishments. There was a fire at the barn that night which destroyed the barn and everything in it. I have since researched into the goings-on in the barn and discovered that they had been experimenting with chemical antidotes and vaccines on military personnel. These men and women had volunteered to be guinea pigs, allowing themselves to be infected by the infectious bronchitis virus, or IBV, from chickens, and then be subjected to all manner of testing to find cures or vaccinations. Today we know this type of virus more commonly as SARS.

"What I also found out was that some of the chemicals used had leaked into the local water stream a few weeks before the fire, and that is why I believe we all had flu in the spring term of school."

"There's been no mention of this at all by the locals," said Robert.

"There won't be. The fire destroyed what evidence was there," replied Alan.

"How did you find out about what was going on?" asked Andrew.

"I found a report on Tu Skreen Lee's desk, describing the experiments being carried out and how the success of the vaccines was short-lived, due to the mutation of one of the viruses into different strains.

"Lee has since used the findings of the report, added them to my exploratory work and has proclaimed that he has developed a vaccine for SARS and MERS. This vaccine doesn't work! Now he knows that I have told my peers at Public Health England this, he wants to silence me, I'm sure of it."

"So, do you think that the information inside of the envelope has anything to do with what you have told us?" asked Andrew.

"I don't know," Alan replied, "there's only one person now, who can tell us that."

****

Opening the rear door to the corridor which led to the office suite, Rosemary noticed how dark it was, when the office was empty.

She unlocked the office door and found herself shouldering the door open against the pile of post, which had been rammed through the letterbox. Forcing the door open, Rosemary stepped into the dark room, leaving Paulina on guard outside. The blinds had been closed tight, allowing just a few streaks of light to hit the carpeted floor. Rosemary stepped over to the window and peered through the bent blades to see that several reporters were talking amongst themselves, waiting for their chance to scoop the latest photo or comment from anyone approaching the front door to the private investigator's office.

Returning to the open door, she gathered up the various letters and parcels and left the room, locking the door behind her.

Chapter 29

"What do you know about Rosemary Chandler?" Robert asked Alan.

"Nothing more than Trevor's parents told Miss Embling that Mrs Chandler would know what to do when she received the envelope," replied Alan.

Robert glanced over at DCI Peter Jones and then at Andrew Braithwaite.

"Do you know how Trevor's parents know Rosemary Chandler, Alan?" asked Robert.

"No, not exactly. I heard that some time ago, that she was the police officer involved with the investigation of a raid on Trubshore's Jewellery Store in Seaford, and that she was the one who had diverted pointing fingers away from an innocent couple who had been accused of the robbery, to the actual perpetrators. Apparently, the innocent couple were close friends of the Johnson's," replied Alan. "That's all I know."

"We happen to know Mrs Chandler, Alan, so I suggest we arrange for you both to meet up and then we can hopefully get to the bottom of why your school friends have been, and continue to be, targeted," DCI Jones said, looking to Robert and Andrew for their acceptance. "In the meantime, we need you to stay here for your own safety, but of course, that is up to you. You are free to leave at any time, however, we cannot guarantee your safety if you decide to leave."

"I'm happy to wait here for Mrs Chandler," Alan replied.

****

It was late into Saturday evening by the time Robert Fox, Rosemary Bennett and Alan Field had been introduced to each other and were now sitting around the oblong gloss white table in the lounge at Robert's safe house.

DCI Peter Jones and Andrew Braithwaite had departed once Robert had returned with Rosemary, both Peter and Andrew assuring them all that the house would be watched over until the morning.

Sitting at the dining table with Robert and Alan, she rifled through the shopping bag of a post, pulling out a large brown paper package and a scrapbook.

"Robert, John must have had this package delivered on the night we left him, according to the delivery label on it," Rosemary said.

Alan immediately recognised the sepia-coloured scrapbook next to it.

"Is that scrapbook mine?"

Rosemary pulled out another envelope from her bag, taking out another scrapbook.

"No, this one is yours."

She passed it over the table to Alan.

Opening the cover, he stared at the full-length photo of himself, standing in his school uniform, in front of the school's main entrance door.

Rosemary opened the front cover of the scrapbook in front of her to see John Branning standing in his school uniform, in the same location.

She took out her iPad, opened the photos section and scanned the photos she had taken over the last few days.

The first image of Derek from his scrapbook was the same as it was for Trevor's.

"Who took these photos, Alan?"

"The school photographer, as far as I remember."

Rosemary turned the page of John's, and Alan did the same.

The image was of John, as a boy, standing in his swimming trunks, by the old open-air swimming pool in Lewes.

Alan's second page was the same as was Derek's too.

Rosemary continued through the pages, comparing the images with those in Alan's scrapbook, as well as the photos taken of Derek's and Trevor's.

"You thought this scrapbook was yours, didn't you, Alan?" asked Rosemary.

"I did, because of its cover," Alan replied, "I haven't seen this for years. Never knew my mother still had it."

"They are all the same," remarked Robert, "which suggests that either the parents collaborated in their design, or that they were put together by one person."

"I think I can help you there," Alan said, picking up on Robert's comment.

"I remember the headmaster sitting with mother in the lounge, with the scrapbook laid over their laps, turning the pages as they looked through the photos."

"Did this happen on a regular basis, Alan?" asked Rosemary.

"Every couple of weeks or so," Alan replied, "that was until just before my sixth birthday."

Rosemary quickly scanned the photos on her iPad and the pages in John's scrapbook.

"Would that be the time when the photos would have gone missing from the scrapbook, Alan?"

Alan turned the pages until he reached the first empty page. He looked across at Rosemary and the empty page in the scrapbook that she was viewing. He turned back the page to the previous photo, casting his mind back to the afternoon when the five boys sat in a circle with their headmaster, on Brighton promenade lapping up the ice cream.

He looked over at Rosemary, who was looking at the same photo.

"These were happy times," Alan recollected, "when we were all together."

"Who was behind the camera, taking the photo, Alan?"

"Miss Embling. She and the headmaster went everywhere together. She took all these photos up until this point."

"Why are the photos missing after this, Alan, until here, where they continue?"

"I'm not sure, but I do know that in my album, the next photo was taken by mother on my ninth birthday."

Robert intervened. "That means that at the time the photos went missing from the albums, Derek died, and the headmaster disappeared."

"This explains why Derek's album is totally empty from this point onwards," responded Rosemary.

"So where are the missing photos?" asked Alan.

Laying her hand on the package in front of her, Rosemary said, "We need to find out what is in this envelope."

****

The bar and lounge at the Watford Colosseum were slowly dispersing of people as they made their way back to their seats for the final performance of the popular classical music concert from the BBC orchestra, featuring Kimberley Honisett, prior to their world tour.

Charlotte Embling was grateful that the passenger lift had been fixed following its breakdown the previous day when she had to endure the stairs to the entrance to the Circle seating area.

She took her place in the middle seat of the front row when her mobile silently buzzed in her bag. She fumbled for it, grabbed it quickly, and pushed the side button, ceasing the incoming call.

"Not again," she muttered to herself as she turned her head to her right, to apologise to the woman next to her.

Her eyes opened wide, the expression on her face was of shock. "What are you doing here?" Charlotte questioned, "You weren't here before the interval."

She was interrupted. "No, I wasn't. However, the lady who was here suddenly felt unwell, poor thing," came the reply. "Let me take that from you Charlotte, so it doesn't disturb anyone anymore." The phone was grabbed from her hand.

Charlotte was visibly shaking.

"It was you at my home the other night, wasn't it?" Charlotte exclaimed as she realised who had whispered her name from the bushes outside of her bungalow.

"Where is the envelope, Charlotte?"

"What envelope?"

"Don't play games with me, Charlotte. I want the envelope," came the menacing reply.

Charlotte smiled back at her. "You will never get your hands on it, nor the information inside to which you seek," Charlotte responded, a sound of resolution in her voice.

"Then there is nothing much more to say, Charlotte," the woman said with a broad smile, as she looked at the screen on Charlotte's phone light up, as it buzzed again, revealing the caller's name and number. "What's your passcode Charlotte?"

"I'm not telling you. Give me back my phone," Charlotte requested quietly, not wanting to cause a scene.

"Goodbye, Charlotte."

Charlotte felt a sharp jab at the top of her thigh. She grimaced in pain before suddenly feeling a wave of nausea, her heart beating slower and harder, her surroundings in front of her eyes quickly becoming a blur, then her eyes began to close, slowly.

"I wonder, just maybe…" said the woman to herself, as she positioned the iPhone under Charlotte's hand, pushing her thumb onto the logic ID button, the fingerprint, unlocking the device.

The woman gently tipped Charlotte's head back, to prevent her body from slumping forward, Charlotte remaining upright in her seat, and the woman got up and left, just as the lights dimmed and the orchestra's kettle drums resounded with a slow rhythmic beat.

In the car park at the rear of the Colosseum, the woman made a call on Charlotte's phone to the police announcing that a woman was dead at the Watford Colosseum, then cut the call. She then pushed the voicemail button and listened to the last message, cut the call, then punched another number into her phone.

"It's me. I know where the envelope is."

****

Kimberley Honisett's mobile rang in the dressing room, as Kimberley was welcomed on stage. She looked up in the direction of the Circle, not realising that her former teacher wasn't looking back at her, then took her seat in front of the piano keyboard. Kimberley focused her eyes on the musical score in front of her and expertly danced her fingers across the polished ivories.

****

It was just ten minutes into the concert, that the bright lights suddenly energised, flooding the Circle of Watford Colosseum's concert hall with the bright white light, as police officers rushed down the steps from the back of the hall to the ends of the front row, beckoning the audience on the first three rows to leave their seats. Rubbing their eyes to adjust to the brightness, the members of the audience hurriedly gathered their possessions and made for the exits.

The rest of the audience followed, the police officers filtering each row out in turn.

The conductor, having been given the order to stop the orchestra, raised his baton swiftly upright, bringing the music to an abrupt halt. Kimberley Honisett looked towards the conductor, then saw the commotion in the front of the Circle where she knew that Charlotte was seated.

"Charlotte," she called out from her seat, as she raised herself up from her piano stool.

The signal was given by the officer in charge that the hall was safe, and Kimberly was escorted off the stage by two of the officers, along the back of house corridor, and into the foyer, pushing through the throng of people exiting down the stairs from the Circle.

"Excuse me, excuse me," Kimberley cried out as she grabbed hold of the handrail pulling herself up the stairs, till she reached the landing, where she was met outside of the double doors to the entrance to the Circle, by two policemen.

"Are you Kimberly Honisett?" the officer asked.

Kimberley nodded.

"Come with me. Charlotte is asking for you, Miss Honisett."

He led her down the steps to the front row of seating and along to where Charlotte was seated, her head supported by the paramedic behind.

"Kimberley, in my bag, there's a card for Rosemary Bennett with her number on it. I sent the envelope to her. I want you to ring her to tell her that she is in danger. Do it now, please, promise me."

"I promise, but from who, Charlotte?" Kimberley asked.

Charlotte smiled at her briefly, then closed her eyes and took her last breath.

****

At the safe house, Rosemary, Robert, and Alan sat around the table, staring at the wording on the brown envelope in front of Rosemary.

Across the top of the envelope, it read Her Majesty's Stationary Office. "I remember these envelopes," said Alan, "Trevor's father had a pile of these in the back room of the pub."

"Did he work for the government?" asked Robert, "I, too remember seeing these when I first joined the Service."

"I don't know, Robert."

Rosemary turned the envelope over and prised open the flap.

"It looks like it has been opened before, Alan," Rosemary said, "you haven't seen inside it before, have you?"

"No, I didn't even want to, not after Trevor's warning to me," replied Alan.

"What did Trevor tell you, Alan?" Rosemary asked.

"Trevor told me that when he had received the envelope from Miss Embling, she told him that she couldn't keep it for any longer, and she didn't want anyone finding it at her home, when she was gone."

"Did she mean when she died."

"He said that when she told him what to do, it was like her last will and testament, to him. She also told him that she knew that there were people inside and from outside of the village who would do anything to get their hands on it, and it seems from the tragic events over last few weeks, that she was right."

Rosemary slipped her hand inside the bulky envelope and pulled out a letter, passing it over to Alan.

"This is from Miss Embling," he said, as he scanned the letter quickly. "If it's okay, I shall read it to you."

He didn't wait for a reply, he read the letter out loud.

My Heroes,

It falls upon me to bring you the news that I have known your secret for many years.

I'm telling you this now because I, myself, am in ill health and I cannot take this to my grave without telling you what I know.

I have watched, with admiration, you all forge your careers from afar and I have shamefully kept this secret to protect you all because I want no harm to come to you.

I ask one thing only, that when you all see the contents, that only you decide what happens to them.

I trust that you will all make the right decision.

My love to you all,

Miss Embling (Charlotte)

Alan placed the letter on the table and tipped out the contents.

In front of them on the table were photos of Trevor, John, and Derek naked, posing in a long mirror, their faces glum. Behind them were the reflections of a man, the same man, sitting on a bed, in his underpants, taking their individual photographs. Rosemary focused on the face behind the camera. It wasn't just any man; it was a man she and Alan both knew, the face in the mirror's reflection was of the headmaster, Peter Dennett.

Chapter 30

The paramedic shook her head.

"Charlotte's gone," she confirmed, and left Kimberley by her side.

Kimberley wept as she held Charlotte's hand. She searched for Charlotte's phone, on her lap, in her bag and on the floor, but couldn't find it.

"Something's not right," she said to the paramedic, "she never loses her phone, she has the strap around her wrist so that she doesn't drop it. Yet, it's not here."

"She may have dropped it."

"It isn't here, I tell you."

The officer standing behind Kimberley heard her comment and placed his hand on her shoulder. Kimberly turned and craned her neck to look up at him.

"We'll conduct a search immediately after we've taken care of Charlotte, Miss Honisett, but first we need to move her."

Coaxing her away from Charlotte's side, he led Kimberley to the exit doors and down into the lobby.

"I need my phone, it's in my dressing room. Can I get it?"

He nodded and escorted her to her room.

She grabbed her phone from the dressing table and read the number of the missed call received earlier; the same number she had been begged to ring. She made the call.

****

Rosemary grabbed the phone on hearing the ringtone. It was Kimberley's number. She answered immediately.

"Miss Bennett, Kimberley Honisett here. Charlotte has asked me to warn you that the contents of the package she sent you, has put you in great danger."

"Is Charlotte there? Can I talk to her, Kimberley?"

"She's dead."

"How, Kimberley?"

"I don't know. They are moving here from her seat now."

"Her seat? Where are you, Kimberley?"

The phone went dead.

****

"Robert, it was Kimberley. Charlotte's dead and she says that we are in danger too."

"Gather everything up, Rose, and I'll get you both to a safe place."

"What about you?"

"I will take care of everything, don't worry, Rose."

Alan scooped up the photos, and Rosemary grabbed the brown envelope and scrapbooks from the table.

"Hold on, Robert. There's something hidden in the cover of this scrapbook," she said, prising the sepia cover off John Branning's photo album.

She teased her hand inside, grabbing at two folded brown envelopes, then placing them onto the table. She opened the first. Inside, there were deeds to a plot of land, a will, and two pieces of paper. On one, it read, 'I repent my sins'. She opened the second. There was another letter, a press cutting and three photos of different women, in stages of undress. She recognised the first, that of Jean Manville lying on the kitchen table, another lying naked on a bed, the third woman posing naked, leaning against the trunk of a tree. It was Trevor's mother.

She unfolded the press cutting, which was from a centre page pull-out from the Sussex Times, which showed Jean Manville standing proudly on the stage with a rosette pinned to her dress. Rosemary unclipped the cutting and passed it over to Alan.

"I remember when she won this rosette," Alan recollected, "it was the first day that I had ever heard my mother and father really argue. I have never seen him so angry."

"Rose, Alan, we need to go now."

Rose nodded. She placed all the newfound items into the envelope and watched as Alan cradled the press cutting against his chest.

"Alan, let's go."

Robert escorted Rose and Alan to a ground floor panic room that he had constructed shortly after purchasing the house, whilst texting a message on his iPhone. He stopped them both in front of the door, raised his right index finger to his lips to direct them to be silent, then raised the lit screen in front of them to convey the instructions that he had just written.

They both nodded, stepped inside the windowless room, and closed and locked the door behind him.

****

Robert punched in the number for DCI Peter Jones. It was answered on the second ring.

"Peter, I need a favour. We've just been told that Charlotte Embling is dead. She's with Kimberley Honisett in Watford, by all accounts. Could you check for me Peter because I believe Rosemary may be next?"

"I'll make a few calls and I shall let you know. In the meantime, I shall ensure that the watch I put on the safe house hasn't been removed, Robert."

"Thanks, Peter, I owe you."

The phone line went dead.

****

Rosemary sat at the table opposite Alan in the windowless room. She had never been in a panic room before and sensed the absolute quiet. She opened the letter she had found in the scrapbook, with a monochrome portrait photograph of Peter Dennett, proudly sporting his mortarboard squarely on his head. He was smiling directly into the lens; his mesmerising eyes were captivating to those looking at him. She read it to herself and then handed it to Alan, who read it aloud.

My Heroes,

The person that you see in the photograph is your Primary School Headmaster, Peter Dennett, and the man whom I loved and adored from afar, every day at school. All the women in Plumpton Green and surrounding villages adored this sophisticated, enigmatic, handsome man, but he had a dark secret, a side to him that I was not aware of, until I found these.

182

I can only apologise to you all for not protecting you and your families against this evil man, whom I now despise. His monstrous acts left me loathing men like him, and believe me, boys, there are plenty like him in this world.

Please forgive me.

Miss Embling (Charlotte)

She watched Alan place the news cutting and photos one by one on the small table beside him.

"Why didn't I see the pain my family and friends were suffering at the hands of this man?" Alan asked.

"You were too young, Alan," Rosemary replied, "I am sorry that you have had to harbour your trauma for all this time."

"I didn't know that Derek and Trevor had endured the abuse at the hands of this man, as well," he said, pointing to the headmaster's photo.

"You've all suffered, Alan, and someone else knows what you have all been through, too, and they don't want the world knowing what has happened to you."

"My friends have died because of this?"

"It's the only possible explanation," Rosemary suggested, closely inspecting the piece of paper glued to the back of the document. She watched Alan bury his head in his hands. "I'm sorry, Alan."

Her eyes focused on the sheen on the back of the deeds. She held the deeds up to the bright light above the table, read the message in neat italic writing on the glued paper, then smiled to herself.

"I believe we've found your Headmaster, Jayne," she said, quietly to herself.

"Let's see what we have here, Alan," Rosemary said, refocusing his attention on the documents on the table.

Turning the document over, Rosemary opened the deeds and the will, placing them alongside each other.

"I recognise the land on the deeds," Alan said, turning it to face her. "This land was once owned by Derek's parents until they sold it to pay for their new sheds on their farm in the sixties. This is where the barns were located, where we first saw the 'spacemen'."

183

Chapter 31

The Yamaha motorcycle slowly pulled out of the junction from Beacon Road, into Carlton Road, the leather-clad motorcyclist scanning the area, searching for movement in and around the parked cars, houses, and bungalows in the road. She clocked her target address was ahead to her left and Robert Fox's Ford Galaxy was parked outside. The rider suddenly spotted the familiar Range Rover just beyond, parked at the junction of Carlton Road and Westdown Road. The man she saw seated in the car behind the wheel was scanning the area around the front of the safe house. The rider rode past the empty police car and stopped behind the Range Rover. She dismounted and walked towards the driver's door.

The driver recognised the rider's gait and lowered the window, poking his head out and turning his head to the rear of the vehicle.

"Boss," the driver greeted, surprised to see the rider.

The rider didn't answer, but swiftly swung her right arm up and pointed the Sure-fire 9 suppressed handgun at the driver's head, unleashing one shot.

The driver had no time to react.

The bullet hit him centre point between the eyes, jolting his head back inside of the car. She walked up to the open window and saw the driver's lifeless body with the bullet hole in the centre of his forehead.

Without a word, the rider walked calmly back to the motorbike, took off the helmet, then turned to face the house. Looking left and right, she checked on the surroundings. There was nothing but silence.

****

Trish Berry was hidden behind the flint wall, watching the fatal shooting from the opposite side of the road. The rider's face was now illuminated by the streetlight above, and Trish heard the woman make the call.

"I'm here at the house and the envelope must be inside. It will be in your hands tonight."

Trish waited until the woman crossed the road, then made the call.

****

Robert took the call.

"Trish."

"Robert," Trish whispered, "it's the same woman who bowled me over at the bungalow in Piddinghoe, and she's on her way to you now. My colleague is in the rear garden. He will cover your back."

"Trish, I owe you," Robert replied.

"She spoke to someone on the phone, Robert, letting them know about an envelope."

"Got that," replied Robert.

"I shall let the team know," Trish concluded.

The line went dead.

Robert unlocked and pulled open the drawer below the tabletop, and grabbed his comms headset from it, then closed the drawer. He switched the headset on.

****

The woman in the leather motorcycle gear finished her call and stood still, taking in her surroundings. Not a sound could be heard.

A movement to her left caught her eye. She stood motionless, waiting to see the movement again. *There*, she thought. She darted to her left, bounding over a flint stonewall, landing on the soft wet ground which cushioned her feet hitting the ground. She crouched low, waiting for the next movement of the person she knew was was now in front of her.

The figure rose slowly and quietly, her head turning from right to left, scanning the area.

"You've lost me, haven't you?" the woman said to herself.

She raised her firearm, took aim and pulled the trigger.

Trish Berry's side of the head exploded as the bullet left her skull. She sank to the ground with a dull thud.

The woman stood motionless as she saw the body slump out of sight.

Turning her head to get a clearer vision of the house, the woman saw movement behind the curtains in the hallway, then a tall figure appeared from the front door.

She needed to get closer for a clear shot.

Her phone buzzed. She clicked the button and raised the device to her ear, listening to the caller's message.

She didn't give an answer, she didn't need to; her goal was clear. She replaced the phone in her pocket and crept twenty paces forward through the undergrowth towards the side of the house. The man was in range, her senses heightened, and she raised her gun, taking aim at the large chest.

****

Robert stood motionless, listening through his headset to the caller.

"ETA, five minutes, Robert."

"Don't think we have that long. Trish is not responding."

"Hang in there, Robert," came the reply, "We're making a silent approach."

The caller hung up.

He detected a movement, slight, to his left, but it was there. He moved back towards the door, just as the side of his body armour was slammed by a heavy blow, knocking him off his feet.

He grabbed the left side of his chest as he fell to the floor, his head hitting the jamb of the door, knocking the headset off into the driveway. He turned his head to see where his headset was, only to view a black boot, for an instant before it connected with his jaw, knocking him unconscious.

****

The woman recognised the headset instantly, picked it up and standing over the limp, still body in the doorway, switched the channels, listening for open feeds.

She smiled to herself, recognising the woman's voice on channel six.

She muted the microphone but kept her ear tuned into the conversation, as she began searching the house.

****

Rosemary reading upside down, clocked the new owner's identity on the deeds.

"It looks like Peter Dennett was the new owner then. He was a landowner as well as a headmaster."

"I told Robert earlier about the barns and how Tu Skreen Lee had falsified the evidence of the experiments that were carried out here."

"What experiments?"

"The ones that killed Derek and his father."

"So, it wasn't his heart?"

"No, I researched this site years ago whilst I was working for Tu Skreen Lee. When I found out about this laboratory, I tackled Tu Skreen Lee on it, only for him to threaten me. I just haven't been able to prove it."

Rosemary opened the envelope marked 'Top Secret', took it out and unfolded the letter, reading the content.

"Until now. This letter from the Home Office must have found its way into the old headmaster's hands, all those years ago."

"So why didn't he report it, Rosemary."

"He did try using the school magazine, but it was confiscated by the MOD before it could be read by anyone."

"He still could have reported it."

"I don't think he could. Perhaps they persuaded him to keep quiet."

"How?" asked Alan.

"They knew of his extra-curricular activities probably, and so threatened to expose him, and of course, ruin him financially, by telling everyone about the worthless piece of land that he had recently bought."

"But the land is prime real estate."

"It is now, Alan, but then it would have been classified as contaminated waste ground. Today, land like this can be treated before developing the site into a housing estate."

"It must be worth over a million pounds."

"In Plumpton, near to the train station, which is on route to London, much more I would suggest."

"So, who stands to benefit, Rosemary?"

Rosemary turned and read the page.

"I think we have found your friends' killer."

****

The woman heard every word.

She had scanned the house, top to bottom, but nobody was there.

I've been duped, she thought.

She took the phone from her pocket and made the call.

"It's not here, nobody is here."

"It must be," the voice replied. "Look, I'm nearly home. I'll call you then."

The phone fell silent.

The woman turned her head towards the door. The man she had shot and kicked unconscious had gone. Panic set in. How could she have been so foolish?

She raised her gun, scanning the area, whilst listening for movement. There was none.

****

Robert felt water splashing over his face. His senses were suddenly alert.

"Robert, it's Peter. Robert?"

"Where's Rose, Peter?"

"She's still inside Robert."

"My headset?"

"The woman has it. Don't worry. We are closing in on her now."

"Here's a transcript of what's been said so far."

Robert read it.

"She's not working alone, Peter."

"We traced the call. It will all be over soon. Thanks for the heads up, Robert."

****

The woman sensed that she was trapped. The only option for her now was to make a dash for freedom. She stepped out of the front door, checking for any movement, and was about to leap over the flint wall in front of her when suddenly, a figure in black battle fatigue appeared to her left from behind the flint wall, pointing the barrel of his semi-automatic directly at her. "Police. Lay down your weapon on the ground."

Her eyes scanned both left and right to see another three officers join the first, all pointing their weapons towards her.

The woman stood still and stared straight ahead as she contemplated her next move. She knew that she had no escape and slowly bent forward placing the handgun on the ground, knowing the drill and before another order was barked at her, she stepped back and lowered herself onto her knees, then onto her front and splayed her arms outstretched to each side of her body.

The police rushed forward in unison, one placing her wrists in cuffs behind her back, whilst another grabbed the gun, making it safe.

The residents from the nearby properties came scurrying out onto the road from their houses, all looking towards the armed police surrounding the lone body on the ground.

"Get back inside your homes and lock your doors," shouted one of the policemen, sending them scurrying back to the houses.

Tears ran down the woman's face as she laid, pinned down to the ground, by the arresting officer. "Sorry Mum," she quietly cried to herself.

****

Robert could hear the commotion through the open comms as he sat in the van.

The 'all clear' was given to his two guests in the panic room, and Rosemary Bennett soon joined him.

"I told Alan to wait in the room, Robert."

"Good call, Rose."

"The woman they have arrested is in the back of the van, Robert."

They walked to the rear of the police van and saw the handcuffed woman through the black grilled door securing her in the van.

"Hello Robert, we meet again."

Rosemary immediately recognised the prisoner.

"Hello, Rachel," replied Robert.

"You don't seem surprised to see me, Robert?"

"I'm not, Rachel. Andrew warned me that you were a loose cannon and when we met on the Pier, the other day, I figured something wasn't right. I just couldn't put my finger on it."

"So, it was you that asked Andrew Braithwaite to send me up north, after Alan, when he was elsewhere."

"Yes." He smiled at her.

"Where is he now, Robert?"

"He's safe," replied Robert, "as is the envelope that you were after."

Rachel looked directly at Rosemary. "I should have got to you earlier, when I had the chance, and not entrusted Walker to finish the job for me. If you need a job done properly, do it yourself, don't you agree, Miss Bennett?"

She pressed her head up to the grilled door and with a smile on her face she said, "When I get released, Robert."

****

The motorbike slowly weaved through the stationary traffic, going south, down the A23. The rider could see the blue flashing lights as she rounded the blind corner towards the Hassocks' turn-off. Two police motorcycles drew up behind her. The rider hadn't seen them beforehand, and she was now worried about their close presence and could sense that they may be closing in on her.

She stopped behind the cue of stationary vehicles in front of her and swung her head from side to side to see the police motorcyclists stop on either side of her.

She could feel the tension rising inside her and considered her options. She knew that she wasn't as proficient as Rachel was on her motorbike. Here and now, she knew that she would be outsmarted by the highly trained riders on either side of her.

Without warning, the bikes speed off, their sirens and blue lights flashing, leaving her alone.

The outer lane cleared, allowing traffic to pass by, so she steered her bike into the fast lane and followed the rubberneckers in front of her, in their cars and vans, looking over to the two stationary vehicles entangled with each other on the inside lane, then she quickly sped off as the highway in front of her cleared, towards Brighton.

Thirty minutes later, the remote-controlled up-and-over garage door opened and her motorcycle inched its way into the empty garage.

The owner dismounted, took off her helmet, placed it on the seat and walked out the garage towards her front door. She depressed the remote control and the garage door closed shut.

The road outside of her home was silent.

Returning the control fob to her left-hand jacket pocket, she zipped the pocket closed and then unzipped her right-hand pocket, took out the house door keys, ready to unlock the door.

"Stand still and spread your arms out to your side," the armed policeman shouted from behind her. She did as she was told.

"Turn around and face me, keeping your arms outstretched," came the second command.

She slowly turned around to face the policeman giving the orders, then two further armed policemen appeared from behind the bushes in the garden, in battle fatigue, pointing their firearms at her. "Lay down on the ground, hands in front of you, where I can see them," the policeman in the centre commanded.

She did as she was ordered and then stayed still, as the policemen cautiously approached her, the one in the centre striding around to her side, kneeling on her back, he pulled her arms behind her, placing handcuffs around both wrists.

"Abigail Wilton, you are under arrest for the murder of Trevor and Louise Johnson, Jean Manville and Charlotte Embling. You do not have to say anything, but anything you do say—"

Abigail drowned out the obligatory caution with her loud scream. "You will all pay for this, I promise you."

Chapter 32

Robert Fox and Rosemary Bennett looked out over Brighton Marina, from the bar terrace of the Malmaison Hotel, watching the masts of the yachts swaying gently in the warm breeze. Robert was impeccably dressed for the occasion in his favourite Tom Ford grey pinstripe suit. Rosemary had treated herself to a mid-length pleated dress.

"I must say, you look stunning, Miss Bennett," the familiar male voice complimented her from behind them.

Robert and Rosemary both turned around to see Alan Manville standing behind them.

"Thank you, Alan, I'm glad somebody noticed," Rosemary replied, turning her head slightly, raising her eyebrows at Robert.

"I couldn't agree more," Robert responded, smiling back at her.

"Can I introduce you to Kimberley Honisett? She's been wanting to meet you both," said Alan.

Kimberley was very tall, towering above Rosemary by more than six inches.

Kimberley was dressed in a Zimmerman mid-length pleated dress. The hem stopped just above the knee of her long legs, exposing her lightly tanned covered shapely calves below.

Kimberley stepped forward and shook hands with Rosemary, who felt the vice-like grip around hers.

"I caught sight of you at the funerals," Rosemary remarked, breaking the ice, and although we crossed messages on the phone, "I'm sorry I haven't had the pleasure of meeting you before now."

"I'm sorry too," replied Kimberley, "I couldn't bring myself to mingle within the congregations at any of the funerals, not even Charlotte's."

Kimberley released her grip from Rosemary's hand and switched her attention to Robert.

"And I've heard only good things about you, Mr Fox," Kimberley said, shaking hands with him, with the same steely grip.

"Call me Robert, please," Robert replied, "and I am honoured to be in the presence of a world-renowned and very attractive pianist."

"You're making me blush, Robert," Kimberley replied, "sorry that I've come unannounced, but I just had to meet you both."

"It's an unexpected pleasure, isn't it, Rose?" Robert replied, smiling at her.

"Ever the charmer, Robert," Rosemary replied, smiling back at him.

"I can see you make a great team," Kimberley said to the private investigators.

"You have some information; I'm led to believe. Let's grab a table over there," Alan said, pointing at the empty table to the end of the balcony, "and you can tell us what you have found."

Rosemary nodded in agreement.

"I would like our client to join us if that's okay?" asked Rosemary. I thought it best for all of us to meet today.

"Not at all. Who's joining us?"

On cue, Jayne Sargeant walked into view. Rosemary beckoned her over.

"Let me introduce you to Derek's stepsister, Jayne. I wanted her to meet you, Alan, and of course, you Kimberley," replied Rosemary.

The three women took their seats next to each other, around a large circular glass top covered wicker table, and Robert heard the start of the conversation, as he headed towards the bar with Alan.

"Alan was one my best friend at school. He looked out for me all those years ago and since we've met again, he has become my soulmate," Kimberley said to Jayne.

Rose saw Kimberley glance over to Alan and then winked at him, just as he turned his head towards her, and he winked back, then blew her a kiss.

Retuning her attention to Rosemary, Kimberley asked, "Do you mind if I call you Rose? It's such a pretty name."

"Not at all."

****

"It's great to see you and Kimberley together, after all this time," Robert said, as they reached the bar.

"I'm accompanying Kimberley on her next world tour, it seems that we have a lot to catch up on, and I shall see America like I have always wanted to, however, now I shall be in just the best company."

****

"We're going to America," said Kimberley to Rosemary and Jayne.

"Is that for business or pleasure?" Jayne enquired.

"A bit of both," replied Kimberley, "Alan has always wanted to visit the USA, and I have been asked to play at twelve venues over there, so we thought of combining the two."

Robert and Alan returned to the table with two trays of drinks.

"Cheers everyone." said Robert, chinking his glass with everyone around the table.

"Now, down to business," he continued, placing his glass on the table, then reaching down beside his seat, he grabbed the box file and placed it in front of him on the table.

"Jayne, you wanted to know more about the disappearance of the headmaster," said Robert. "What we have found is likely to stir emotions which may be hurtful to all of you…"

"Robert, I need closure on this, so please, so long as Alan and Kimberley are in agreement, we would like to know everything," replied Jayne.

"Alan and I are with you on this, Jayne. It's been too long now not knowing what happened all those years ago," Kimberley agreed.

"Well, first and foremost, all of the evidence gathered here in this file" – Robert commented, placing his hand on the red box file in front of him – "suggests that Peter Dennett did commit suicide. From the information that we found in the scrapbooks and envelopes, Charlotte Embling and he were once lovers, for around four years, but when she found out about his sordid antics with the mothers of the school children, as well as the children themselves, she turned her back on him. When he knew that Charlotte had found out, he tore this page out of the school diary, writing what looks like his his final message, expecting it to be read once he had gone," Robert said, laying it flat on the table. "Peter's apology to the world," Robert stated, allowing everyone time to read the message written in italics – 'To the person who reads this. I am sorry'.

Rosemary recognised the writing on the paper which had been stuck to the deeds, then saw the date in the top right of the page. It was from Peter Dennett's diary, the same diary that she was shown at Abigail's house. Her eyes focused on the writing again, then she saw the missing corner. She grabbed her handbag and retrieved the triangular piece of paper which Jayne had given to her at their first meeting. She placed it on the table and matched the torn edge to the missing corner of the diary page.

"The headmaster was also saying sorry to your mum too, Jayne," Rosemary said.

"Where did you find the page, Robert?" asked Jayne.

"It had been stuck firmly to the back of the deeds, which Rose found hidden in the cover of John Branning's scrapbook photo album," Robert replied.

He retrieved the letter and deeds from the box file and laid them on the table for them all to see.

"As you can see here," Robert pointed at the letter, "Peter Dennett's signature is here, witnessed by none other than your mother, Alan."

"Is this the reason she was murdered?" Alan asked, staring at his mother's signature.

"Yes, by the headmaster's daughter, Abigail," replied Robert. "She found out about the land, which is to the west of Plumpton Racecourse, during her time as Chair of the Plumpton Historical Society. The will's only beneficiary was Karen Wilton, who he secretly adored. Karen's last will and testament was made out to Keith, who she still believed to be alive, even though she hadn't heard from him for over fifty years and of course, Abigail. Abigail tried in vain to make her mother remove Keith from the will to no avail. Till her death, Karen believed her son to be alive, and no one was going to persuade otherwise. There were now two stumbling blocks for Abigail. One, the original 'last will and testament' written by her father was hidden, as she thought, in the elusive envelope, and two, Keith was in his mother's will.

"In fact, her father had hidden his will in the scrapbook belonging to the Branning family and having scoured records of her stepbrother's existence, she found nothing, so believing that she was the only heir to the land.

"During a conversation that Abigail and I had, whilst investigating her father's disappearance, Abigail told me that she had lost a child," Rosemary interjected, "and she gave everyone the impression that her daughter had died too, whereas, in fact, her daughter was taken from Abigail within six months of her giving birth because the authorities were concerned about the child's safety given that Abigail had twice been admitted into hospital due to self-harming."

"I feel quite sorry for her," said Kimberley, "I wouldn't wish that on anyone, to have your baby taken away, it must have traumatised Abigail."

"It did," replied Robert. "She fought for years to get in touch with her, but the authorities forbade it. I shall come on to what happened between them shortly."

"Regarding Charlotte, she was diagnosed with lung cancer," said Rosemary. "If my timings are correct, she knew about her cancer shortly before she handed the envelope to Trevor. It was her way of trying to put right what had happened when she was a teacher at the school."

Tears welled in Kimberley's eyes. "She kept that from Trevor, John, Alan, and me for all this time?"

Rosemary handed Kimberley a clean tissue from her pocket.

"I'm afraid so," replied Robert. "She kept silent about a great many things, which she made apparent in this letter, along with her last will and testament. I won't go into them now, but I will leave you Jayne, with the box file of letters which you can read with Alan and Kimberley in more private surroundings."

Kimberley nodded. "Thank you, Robert."

"Where does Abigail's daughter fit into this?" Alan asked.

"Our investigations found out that Abigail Wilton married a wealthy man who was twenty years her senior, named Benjamin Stevens." He placed a copy of the marriage certificate on the table in front of him.

"He seemed like the perfect partner for Abigail, giving her everything that she could ever want; plenty of spending money and a child by the name of Rachel Stevens. Benjamin Stevens died in a tragic car accident shortly after Rachel's second birthday. Abigail suffered manic depression as a result and her ability to properly take care of her own child was questioned.

"Rachel, having been taken into care, was adopted by private school teachers, who had educated her well at home and within a state school in Reigate. She went to Cambridge University, where she studied languages, excelling in Middle Eastern dialects. Rachel was recruited by MI6 following her term at Cambridge and this is where she cut her teeth in all matters of security and counter-surveillance.

"She was posted to Iraq between 2005 and 2008, where she assisted in the transcripts of prisoners during interrogations.

"On her way back to the airport, she was captured and tortured for three months until her rescue in early 2009. Rachel left MI6 in 2013, dissatisfied that she had been confined to a desk job in Vauxhall. Her time behind the desk wasn't in vain, though. She spent her time searching out her natural parents and when she resigned from the Service, she set about finding them.

"She quickly learnt about the father who she would never meet and found out all about her mother, eventually meeting Abigail in her home in Plumpton Green. They connected immediately and became very close.

"Abigail told her about the inheritance she sought and what was standing in her way. Rachel explained to her that she had been working for a private security firm, specialising in the extraction of UK and USA citizens who were imprisoned in Iraq and that she had come back to the UK where she was working for several wealthy entrepreneurs, obtaining corporate secrets from their competitors. She realised the huge mutual financial benefit that was being promised to her by Abigail, and so together they executed their plan to find the letter and the land registry deeds, then one by one, removing the opposition, leaving Abigail to become the sole beneficiary, sharing the proceeds equally with herself.

"Nobody connected the two together, I'm afraid, MI5 was even going to engage Rachel to find you, Alan, until I persuaded my old friend from the Department to send her north, giving my colleague and I the chance to take you to a safe house. It was unfortunate that one department didn't talk with the other, because they sent one of Rachel Steven's team, Brad Hammond, to monitor the safe house, not realising that Rachel had trackers on all her team's vehicles. She quickly realised that she was being sent up a blind alley and that you were not up north of the country.

"She was also informed by Abigail that Rose's voicemail to Charlotte confirmed that she was in possession of the envelope in which the letter and deeds were found, and she knew that Rose could have only been on the south coast."

"Abigail and Rachel thought that because of Rachel's background and current position, they were untouchable. How wrong they were," Kimberley said. "Now they are where they belong; behind bars."

Robert placed all the papers back into the box file and slid the box over to Jayne.

"What was the connection with the experiments in the barn in Plumpton and Tu Skreen Lee?" Robert asked Alan, "I have heard that you have been helping my old colleagues in MI5 with much-needed information."

"On matters of national security, I tend not to talk too much, but what I can divulge is that the Ministry of Defence did conduct experiments in the 1960s on land which was compulsorily purchased from the local farming family," Alan replied. "One of their experiments did fail, in that there was a leak from a tank at the barn, causing some pollution of the stream by the school. This resulted in those who drank the water from it suffering from minor breathing problems, causing them bronchial issues. These were short-lived and had no long-lasting effects. For Derek though, he was exposed to the patients who had volunteered to take part in the SARS experiments, losing his life as a result. His family have since been compensated by the MOD."

Alan looked over to Kimberley. "Derek shouldn't have died, and the Ministry of Defence should not have been there in the first place."

"There is one positive side to Peter Dennett though, he did get to know about the experiments being conducted and had the intention of publishing his findings in the school magazine and the local newspaper. Her Majesty's Government got early wind of this and stemmed the publications, using their network of connections to ensure that the unwanted publicity and matters which affected National Security were censored. The barn was torched shortly after the MOD vacated the site" – Alan confirmed, then continued – "Tu Skreen Lee, however, was considered an imminent threat to national security and so was deported from the UK, never to return. His illegal use of mammals and birds to conduct his experiments were considered not only dangerous to the immediate wildlife in the local area, but the entire nation. It was reported that he returned to his post as Chief Virologist in China's leading laboratory in Wuhan."

"I understand that the Government considered that their actions, taken as a result of the information that you provided them, prevented, what could have been, a national catastrophe," remarked Robert. Alan nodded in agreement, and they chinked their beer tankards together.

"I, for one, am very proud of him, Robert," Kimberley said, looking over at Alan.

"Quite right too. It's not what your country can do for you, it's what you can do for your country," replied Robert.

"We met Chloe after John's funeral, poor thing, and then again at a specialist care home for abused women in Horsham," said Kimberley.

"How is she doing?" Rosemary asked.

"She's coping, after all she has been through. She seems to like it at the home, has made friends with a couple of other women of her age and has surprised the staff with her cake making skills. Lemon drizzle is her favourite, apparently. She says that Alan's mother taught her how to make it when she was young."

Rosemary remembered the cake that Jean Manville had given to her before she was murdered but decided not to mention it.

"Her mother is on remand awaiting trial, as are Abigail and Rachel," said Robert.

"I will be honest; we are not looking forward to our past being raked up again for all the world to see. The press are already publishing the story of what happened all those years ago, headlining the story 'The Plumpton Boys', having seen the leaked case files," Alan said, looking over at Kimberley.

"We shall be fine, Alan. Together, we shall be telling the horrid truth about Abigail, Rachel, Deborah Branning, and Peter Dennett." Kimberley responded.

He shrugged his shoulders, then took her hand in his. "Yes, together we will," he replied.

"What about you, Jayne? How do you feel now the truth is out?" asked Robert.

"I'm very happy with what you have told me. My mother's ability to communicate or understand what is happening, God bless her, has deteriorated rapidly, but I am pleased that I am able to tell her she was right all along about Derek's death, and her final wish shall be fulfilled. The Ministry of Defence has made a substantial payment to me for what they did to Derek and his father. It means that mother will get the best possible treatment in the short time that she has left." Jayne turned to face Rosemary directly. "I'm sorry for the things I said to you in the pub."

"There's no need to apologise," Rosemary replied.

"You have both been such great support and extremely conscientious, too. I am aware that I haven't paid you yet for the investigation, so I would like to do that now," said Jayne, handing over a thickly padded envelope.

"And this envelope is from me," Kimberley said, handing over a padded envelope to Rosemary. "It's my thank you for saving Alan's life. Please open it only when we have all left, and we all wish you both well in your future investigations."

"I think that's my cue to say farewell to you, Robert and Rosemary," said Alan.

"Me too," said Jayne. She picked up the box file as they all stood, shook hands with each other, and then Alan, Jayne, and Kimberley left Robert and Rosemary at the table.

They watched them leave through the bar and out of sight.

"Very satisfied customers," remarked Robert, "and it looks like we have been handsomely paid."

"Shall we open them now and see how much is inside?" asked Rosemary.

"No, let's wait until we get back to the office, Rose."

"Why not now, Robert?"

"No, I think we should wait, Rose. I would rather wait and open them in the privacy of our office."

"I could just have a peek," Rosemary said, cheekily.

"I'll do it, Rose," Robert responded, holding out his hand for them.

"Okay," Rosemary said, with a glint in her eye, as she handed them to him. Robert slipped them into his inside jacket pocket.

"I thought that you were going to open them, Robert."

"I shall, when we get back to the office."

"Not now?"

"No, at the office." He stood up and started walking towards the exit door.

"Sometimes, you can be the most annoying—"

"I know, Rose," he replied with a mischievous grin on his face. "Are you coming?"

End